Monkey Trouble and Other Stories

Ruskin Bond is known for his signature simplistic and witty writing style. He is the author of several bestselling short stories, novellas, collections, essays and children's books; and has contributed a number of poems and articles to various magazines and anthologies. At the age of 23, he won the prestigious John Llewellyn Rhys Prize for his first novel, *The Room on the Roof*. He was also the recipient of the Padma Shri in 1999, Lifetime Achievement Award by the Delhi Government in 2012 and the Padma Bhushan in 2014.

Born in 1934, Ruskin Bond grew up in Jamnagar, Shimla, New Delhi and Dehradun. Apart from three years in the UK, he has spent all his life in India and now lives in Landour, Mussoorie, with his adopted family.

RUSKIN BOND

Monkey Trouble and Other Stories

RUPA

Published by
Rupa Publications India Pvt. Ltd 2025
7/16, Ansari Road, Daryaganj
New Delhi 110002

Sales centres:
Bengaluru Chennai
Hyderabad Jaipur Kathmandu
Kolkata Mumbai Prayagraj

P-ISBN: 978-93-7003-642-0
E-ISBN: 978-93-7003-580-5

First impression 2025

10 9 8 7 6 5 4 3 2 1

The moral right of the author has been asserted.

CONTENTS

INTRODUCTION

Much of life in the mountains is spent in close vicinity of wildlife, creatures unknown and known, great and small, skirting the edges of human dwellings. Some of these animals, like the ubiquitous monkeys who steal your food, become friends at best, and nuisances at worst. Others, like tigers or leopards or bears, those fearsome monarchs of the jungle, are best given a wide berth, from where one can safely observe them with the usual mixture of fear, curiosity and awe.

Regardless of all precautions, though, there are moments where the curtain parts, man and the wild coming face to face, and the order of life hangs in the balance for both.

Monkey Trouble and Other Stories brings together a collection of my writings about these moments, and their pleasant and sometimes not-so-pleasant consequences. 'Monkey Trouble' and 'Monkeys in the Loo' are about the humorous situations that can transpire when monkeys come into contact with humans, leaving chaos in their wake in their usual playful yet disruptive manner. 'Exciting Encounters' is about those legendary tales of hunting and hunters that never fail to thrill, while 'No Room for a Leopard' is about the discomfiting feelings that arise when the legend becomes reality, the hunt becoming a killing. 'Romi and the Wildfire' gives a glimpse of what cooperation between humans and wildlife looks like in the face of a bigger threat. In contrast, 'The Tiger in the Tunnel' is about an encounter gone wrong, and how the consequences of the curtain parting too far can often be deadly.

Humans and wildlife have always lived a parallel existence, our chance encounters spelling both joy and sorrow. The more we encroach into their spaces, the more we destabilize that connection. I hope the stories here encourage you to live and let live, and wait for chance to allow us to slip in and out of each other's realms in positive and memorable ways.

Ruskin Bond

MONKEY TROUBLE

Grandfather bought Tutu from a street entertainer for the sum of ten rupees. The man had three monkeys. Tutu was the smallest, but the most mischievous. She was tied up most of the time. The little monkey looked so miserable with a collar and chain that Grandfather decided it would be much happier in our home. Grandfather had a weakness for keeping unusual pets. It was a habit that I, at the age of eight or nine, used to encourage.

Grandmother at first objected to having a monkey in the house. 'You have enough pets as it is,' she said, referring to Grandfather's goat, several white mice and a small tortoise.

'But I don't have any,' I said.

'You're wicked enough for two monkeys. One boy in the house is all I can take.'

'Ah, but Tutu isn't a boy,' said Grandfather triumphantly. 'This is a little girl monkey!'

Grandmother gave in. She had always wanted a little girl in the house. She believed girls were less troublesome than boys. Tutu was to prove her wrong.

She was a pretty little monkey. Her bright eyes sparkled with mischief beneath deep-set eyebrows. And her teeth, which were a pearly white, were often revealed in a grin that frightened the wits out of Aunt Ruby, whose nerves had already suffered from the presence of Grandfather's pet python. But this was my grandparents' house, and aunts and uncles had to put up with our pets.

Tutu's hands had a dried-up look, as though they had been pickled in the sun for many years. One of the first things I taught her was to shake hands, and this she insisted on doing with all who visited the house. Peppery Major Malik would have to stoop and shake hands with Tutu before he could enter the drawing room, otherwise Tutu would climb onto his shoulder and stay there, roughing up his hair and playing with his moustache.

Uncle Benji couldn't stand any of our pets and took a particular dislike to Tutu, who was always making faces at him. But as Uncle Benji was never in a job for long, and depended on Grandfather's good-natured generosity, he had to shake hands with Tutu, like everyone else.

Tutu's fingers were quick and wicked. And her tail, while adding to her good looks (Grandfather believed a tail would add to anyone's good looks!), also served as a third hand. She could use it to hang from a branch, and it was capable of scooping up any delicacy that might be out of reach of her hands.

On one of Aunt Ruby's visits, loud shrieks from her bedroom brought us running to see what was wrong. It was only Tutu trying on Aunt Ruby's petticoats! They were much too large, of course, and when Aunt Ruby entered the room, all she saw was a faceless white blob jumping up and down on the bed.

We disentangled Tutu and soothed Aunt Ruby. I gave Tutu a bunch of sweet peas to make her happy. Granny didn't like anyone plucking her sweet peas, so I took some from Major Malik's garden while he was having his afternoon siesta.

Then Uncle Benji complained that his hairbrush was missing. We found Tutu sunning herself on the back verandah, using the hairbrush to scratch her armpits.

I took it from her and handed it back to Uncle Benji with an apology; but he flung the brush away with an oath.

'Such a fuss about nothing,' I said. 'Tutu doesn't have fleas!'

'No, and she bathes more often than Benji,' said Grandfather, who had borrowed Aunt Ruby's shampoo to give Tutu a bath.

All the same, Grandmother objected to Tutu being given the run of the house. Tutu had to spend her nights in the outhouse, in the company of the goat. They got on quite well, and it was not long before Tutu was seen sitting comfortably on the back of the goat, while the goat roamed the back garden in search of its favourite grass.

The day Grandfather had to visit Meerut to collect his railway pension, he decided to take Tutu and me along to keep us both out of mischief, he said. To prevent Tutu from wandering about on the train, causing inconvenience to passengers, she was provided with a large black travelling bag. This, with some straw at the bottom, became her compartment. Grandfather and I paid for our seats, and we took Tutu along as hand baggage.

There was enough space for Tutu to look out of the bag occasionally, and to be fed with bananas and biscuits, but she could not get her hands through the opening and the canvas was too strong for her to bite her way through.

Tutu's efforts to get out only had the effect of making the bag roll about on the floor or occasionally jump into the air—an exhibition that attracted a curious crowd of onlookers at the Dehra and Meerut railway stations.

Anyway, Tutu remained in the bag as far as Meerut, but while Grandfather was producing our tickets at the turnstile, she suddenly poked her head out of the bag and gave the ticket collector a wide grin.

The poor man was taken aback. But, with great presence of mind and much to Grandfather's annoyance, he said, 'Sir, you have a dog with you. You'll have to buy a ticket for it.'

'It's not a dog!' said Grandfather indignantly. 'This is a baby monkey of the species *macacus mischievous*, closely related to the human species *homus horriblis*! And there is no charge for babies!'

'It's as big as a cat,' said the ticket collector. 'Cats and dogs have to be paid for.'

'But, I tell you, it's only a baby!' protested Grandfather.

'Have you a birth certificate to prove that?' demanded the ticket collector.

'Next, you'll be asking to see her mother,' snapped Grandfather.

In vain did he take Tutu out of the bag. In vain did he try to prove that a young monkey did not qualify as a dog or a cat or even as a quadruped. Tutu was classified as a dog by the ticket collector, and five rupees were handed over as her fare.

Then Grandfather, just to get his own back, took from his pocket the small tortoise that he sometimes carried about, and said: 'And what must I pay for this, since you charge for all creatures great and small?'

The ticket collector looked closely at the tortoise, prodded it with his forefinger, gave Grandfather a triumphant look, and said, 'No charge, sir. It is not a dog!'

•

Winters in North India can be very cold. A great treat for Tutu on winter evenings was the large bowl of hot water given to her by Grandfather for a bath. Tutu would cunningly test the temperature with her hand, then gradually step into the bath, first one foot, then the other (as she had seen me doing) until she was in the water upto her neck.

Once comfortable, she would take the soap in her hands or feet and rub herself all over. When the water became cold, she would get out and run as quickly as she could to the kitchen fire in order to dry herself. If anyone laughed at her during this performance, Tutu's feelings would be hurt and she would refuse to go on with the bath.

One day Tutu almost succeeded in boiling herself alive. Grandmother had left a large kettle on the fire for tea. And Tutu, all by herself and with nothing better to do, decided to remove the lid. Finding the water just warm enough for a bath, she got in, with her head sticking out from the open kettle.

This was fine for a while, until the water began to get heated. Tutu raised herself a little. But finding it cold outside, she sat down again. She continued hopping up and down for some time, until Grandmother returned and hauled her, half-boiled, out of the kettle.

'What's for tea today?' asked Uncle Benji gleefully. 'Boiled eggs and a half-boiled monkey?'

But Tutu was none the worse for the adventure and continued to bathe more regularly than Uncle Benji.

Aunt Ruby was a frequent taker of baths. This met with Tutu's approval—so much so that, one day, when Aunt Ruby had finished shampooing her hair, she looked up through a lather of bubbles and soap suds to see Tutu sitting opposite her in the bath, following her example.

◆

One day Aunt Ruby took us all by surprise. She announced that she had become engaged. We had always thought Aunt Ruby would never marry—she had often said so herself—but it appeared that the right man had now come along in the person of Rocky Fernandes, a schoolteacher from Goa.

Rocky was a tall, firm-jawed, good-natured man, a couple of years younger than Aunt Ruby. He had a fine baritone voice and sang in the manner of the great Nelson Eddy. As Grandmother liked baritone singers, Rocky was soon in her good books.

'But what on earth does he see in her?' Uncle Benji wanted to know.

'More than any girl has seen in you!' snapped Grandmother. 'Ruby's a fine girl. And they're both teachers. Maybe they can start a school of their own.'

Rocky visited the house quite often and brought me chocolates and cashew nuts, of which he seemed to have an unlimited supply. He also taught me several marching songs. Naturally, I approved of Rocky. Aunt Ruby won my grudging admiration for having made such a wise choice.

One day I overheard them talking of going to the bazaar to buy an engagement ring. I decided I would go along, too. But as Aunt Ruby had made it clear that she did not want me around, I decided that I had better follow at a discreet distance. Tutu, becoming aware that a mission of some importance was under way, decided to follow me. But as I had not invited her along, she too decided to keep out of sight.

Once in the crowded bazaar, I was able to get quite close to Aunt Ruby and Rocky without being spotted. I waited until they had settled down in a large jewellery shop before sauntering past and spotting them, as though by accident. Aunt Ruby wasn't too pleased at seeing me, but Rocky waved and called out, 'Come and join us! Help your aunt choose a beautiful ring!'

The whole thing seemed to be a waste of good money, but I did not say so—Aunt Ruby was giving me one of her more unloving looks.

'Look, these are pretty!' I said, pointing to some cheap, bright agates set in white metal. But Aunt Ruby wasn't looking. She was immersed in a case of diamonds.

'Why not a ruby for Aunt Ruby?' I suggested, trying to please her.

'That's her lucky stone,' said Rocky. 'Diamonds are the

thing for engagements.' And he started singing a song about a diamond being a girl's best friend.

While the jeweller and Aunt Ruby were sifting through the diamond rings, and Rocky was trying out another tune, Tutu had slipped into the shop without being noticed by anyone but me. A little squeal of delight was the first sign she gave of her presence. Everyone looked up to see her trying on a pretty necklace.

'And what are those stones?' I asked.

'They look like pearls,' said Rocky.

'They *are* pearls,' said the shopkeeper, making a grab for them.

'It's that dreadful monkey!' cried Aunt Ruby. 'I knew that boy would bring her here!'

The necklace was already adorning Tutu's neck. I thought she looked rather nice in pearls, but she gave us no time to admire the effect. Springing out of our reach, Tutu dodged around Rocky, slipped between my legs, and made for the crowded road. I ran after her, shouting to her to stop, but she wasn't listening.

There were no branches to assist Tutu in her progress, but she used the heads and shoulders of people as springboards and so made rapid headway through the bazaar.

The jeweller left his shop and ran after us. So did Rocky. So did several bystanders who had seen the incident. And others, who had no idea what it was all about, joined in the chase. As Grandfather used to say, 'In a crowd, everyone plays follow-the-leader, even when they don't know who's leading.' Not everyone knew that the leader was Tutu. Only the front runners could see her.

She tried to make her escape speedier by leaping onto the back of a passing scooterist. The scooter swerved into a fruit stall and came to a standstill under a heap of bananas, while the scooterist found himself in the arms of an indignant fruitseller. Tutu peeled a banana and ate part of it, before deciding to move on.

From an awning, she made an emergency landing on a washerman's donkey. The donkey promptly panicked and rushed down the road, while bundles of washing fell by the wayside. The washerman joined in the chase. Children on their way to school decided that there was something better to do than attend classes. With shouts of glee, they soon overtook their panting elders.

Tutu finally left the bazaar and took a road leading in the direction of our house. But knowing that she would be caught and locked up once she got home, she decided to end the chase by ridding herself of the necklace. Deftly removing it from her neck, she flung it in the small canal that ran down the road.

The jeweller, with a cry of anguish, plunged into the canal. So did Rocky. So did I. So did several other people, both adults and children. It was to be a treasure hunt!

Some twenty minutes later, Rocky shouted, 'I've found it!' Covered in mud, water lilies, ferns and tadpoles, we emerged from the canal, and Rocky presented the necklace to the relieved shopkeeper.

Everyone trudged back to the bazaar to find Aunt Ruby waiting in the shop, still trying to make up her mind about a suitable engagement ring.

Finally the ring was bought, the engagement was announced, and a date was set for the wedding.

'I don't want that monkey anywhere near us on our wedding day,' declared Aunt Ruby.

'We'll lock her up in the outhouse,' promised Grandfather. 'And we'll let her out only after you've left for your honeymoon.'

A few days before the wedding I found Tutu in the kitchen, helping Grandmother prepare the wedding cake. Tutu often helped with the cooking and, when Grandmother wasn't looking, added herbs, spices, and other interesting items to the pots—so that occasionally we found a chilli in the custard or an onion in the jelly or a strawberry floating in the chicken soup.

Sometimes these additions improved a dish, sometimes they did not. Uncle Benji lost a tooth when he bit firmly into a sandwich which contained walnut shells.

I'm not sure exactly what went into that wedding cake when Grandmother wasn't looking—she insisted that Tutu was always very well-behaved in the kitchen—but I did spot Tutu stirring in some red chilli sauce, bitter gourd seeds and a generous helping of egg shells!

It's true that some of the guests were not seen for several days after the wedding, but no one said anything against the cake. Most people thought it had an interesting flavour.

The great day dawned, and the wedding guests made their way to the little church that stood on the outskirts of Dehra—a town with a church, two mosques and several temples.

I had offered to dress Tutu up as a bridesmaid and bring her along, but no one except Grandfather thought it was a good idea. So I was an obedient boy and locked Tutu in the outhouse. I did, however, leave the skylight open a little. Grandmother had always said that fresh air was good for growing children, and I thought Tutu should have her share of it.

◆

The wedding ceremony went without a hitch. Aunt Ruby looked a picture, and Rocky looked like a film star.

Grandfather played the organ, and did so with such gusto that the small choir could hardly be heard. Grandmother cried a little. I sat quietly in a corner, with the little tortoise on my lap.

When the service was over, we trooped out into the sunshine and made our way back to the house for the reception.

The feast had been laid out on tables in the garden. As the gardener had been left in charge, everything was in order. Tutu was on her best behaviour. She had, it appeared, used the skylight to avail of more fresh air outside, and now sat beside the three-tier wedding cake, guarding it against crows, squirrels and the goat. She greeted the guests with squeals of delight.

It was too much for Aunt Ruby. She flew at Tutu in a rage. And Tutu, sensing that she was not welcome, leapt away, taking with her the top tier of the wedding cake.

Led by Major Malik, we followed her into the orchard, only to find that she had climbed to the top of the jackfruit tree. From there she proceeded to pelt us with bits of wedding cake. She had also managed to get hold of a bag of confetti, and when she ran out of cake she showered us with confetti.

'That's more like it!' said the good-humoured Rocky. 'Now let's return to the party, folks!'

Uncle Benji remained with Major Malik, determined to chase Tutu away. He kept throwing stones into the tree, until he received a large piece of cake bang on his nose. Muttering threats, he returned to the party, leaving the major to do battle.

When the festivities were finally over, Uncle Benji took the old car out of the garage and drove up the verandah steps. He was going to drive Aunt Ruby and Rocky to the nearby hill resort of Mussoorie, where they would have their honeymoon.

Watched by family and friends, Aunt Ruby climbed into the back seat. She waved regally to everyone. She leant out of the window and offered me her cheek and I had to kiss her farewell. Everyone wished them luck.

As Rocky burst into song, Uncle Benji opened the throttle and stepped on the accelerator. The car shot forward in a cloud of dust.

Rocky and Aunt Ruby continued to wave to us. And so did

Tutu, from her perch on the rear bumper! She was clutching a bag in her hands and showering confetti on all who stood in the driveway.

'They don't know Tutu's with them!' I exclaimed. 'She'll go all the way to Mussoorie! Will Aunt Ruby let her stay with them?'

'Tutu might ruin the honeymoon,' said Grandfather. 'But don't worry—our Benji will bring her back!'

NO ROOM FOR A LEOPARD

I first saw the leopard when I was crossing the small stream at the bottom of the hill. The ravine was so deep that for most of the day it remained in shadow. This encouraged many birds and animals to emerge from cover during the hours of daylight. Few people ever passed that way; only milkmen and charcoal burners from the surrounding villages. As a result, the ravine had become a little haven for wildlife, one of the few natural sanctuaries left near Mussoorie.

Below my cottage was a forest of oak and maple and Himalayan rhododendron. A narrow path twisted its way down through the trees, over an open ridge where red sorrel grew wild, and then down steeply through a tangle of wild raspberries, creeping vines and slender rangal bamboo. At the bottom of the hill, a path led onto a grassy verge surrounded by wild dogroses. The streams ran close by the verge, tumbling over smooth pebbles, over rock worn yellow with age, on its way to the plains and to the little Song River and finally to the sacred Ganga.

Nearly every morning, and sometimes during the day, I heard the cry of the barking deer. And in the evening, walking through the forest, I disturbed parties of kalij pheasants. The birds went gliding into the ravines on open, motionless wings. I saw pine martins and a handsome red fox. I recognized the footprints of a bear.

As I had not come to take anything from the jungle, the birds and animals soon grew accustomed to my face. Or possibly they recognized my footsteps. After some time, my approach did not disturb them. A spotted forktail, which at first used to fly away, now remained perched on a boulder in the middle of the stream while I got across by means of other boulders only a few yards away.

The langurs in the oak and rhododendron trees who would at first go leaping through the branches at my approach, now watched me with some curiosity as they munched on the tender green shoots of the oak. The young ones scuffled and wrestled like boys while their parents groomed each other's coats, stretching themselves out on the sunlit hillside—beautiful animals with slim waists and long sinewy legs and tails full of character. But one evening, as I passed, I heard them chattering in the trees and I was not the cause of their excitement.

As I crossed the stream and began climbing the hill, the grunting and chattering increased, as though the langurs were trying to warn me of some hidden danger. A shower of pebbles came rattling down the steep hillside and I looked up to see a sinewy orange-gold leopard, poised on a rock about twenty feet above me.

It was not looking towards me but had its head thrust attentively forward in the direction of the ravine. It must have sensed my presence because it slowly turned its head and looked down at me. It seemed a little puzzled at my presence there, and when, to give myself courage, I clapped my hands sharply, the leopard sprang away into the thickets, making absolutely no sound as it melted into the shadows. I had disturbed the animal in its quest for food. But a little later, I heard the quickening cry of a barking deer as it fled through the forest—the hunt was still on.

The leopard, like other members of the cat family, is nearing extinction in India and I was surprised to find one so close to Mussoorie. Probably the deforestation that had been taking place in the surrounding hills had driven the deer into this green valley and the leopard, naturally, had followed.

It was some weeks before I saw the leopard again, although I was often made aware of its presence. A dry rasping cough sometimes gave it away. At times I felt certain that I was being followed. And once, when I was late getting home, I was startled by a family of porcupines running about in a clearing. I looked around nervously and saw two bright eyes staring at me from a thicket. I stood still, my heart banging away against my ribs. Then the eyes danced away and I realized they were only fireflies.

In May and June, when the hills were brown and dry, it was always cool and green near the stream where ferns, maidenhair and long grasses continued to thrive.

One day I found the remains of a barking deer that had been partially eaten. I wondered why the leopard had not hidden the remains of his meal and decided that he had been disturbed while eating. Then, climbing the hill, I met a party of *shikaris* resting beneath the oaks. They asked me if I had seen a leopard. I said I had not. They said they knew there was a leopard in the forest. Leopard skins, they told me, were selling in Delhi at over a thousand rupees each! Of course there was a ban on the export of its skins but they gave me to understand that there were ways and means... I thanked them for their information and moved on, feeling uneasy and disturbed.

The shikaris had seen the carcass of the deer and the leopard's pug marks and they kept coming to the forest. Almost every evening I heard their guns banging away, for they were ready to fire at almost everything.

'There's a leopard about,' they told me. 'You should carry a gun.'

'I don't have one,' I said.

There were fewer birds to be seen and even the langurs

had moved on. The red fox did not show itself and the pine martens who had earlier become bold now dashed into hiding at my approach. The smell of one human is like the smell of any other.

I thought no more of the men. My attitude towards them was similar to the attitude of the denizens of the forest—they were men, unpredictable and to be avoided if possible.

One day after crossing the stream, I climbed Pari Tibba, a bleak, scrub-covered hill where no one lived. This was a stiff undertaking, because there was no path to the top and I had to scramble up a precipitous rock-face with the help of rocks and roots which were apt to come away in my groping hand. But at the top was a plateau with a few pine trees, their upper branches catching the wind and humming softly. There I found the ruins of what must have been the first settlers—just a few piles of rubble now overgrown with weeds, sorrel, dandelion and nettles.

As I walked through the roofless ruins, I was struck by the silence that surrounded me, the absence of birds and animals, the sense of complete desolation. The silence was so absolute that it seemed to be shouting in my ears. But there was something else of which I was becoming increasingly aware—the strong feline odour of one of the cat family. I paused and looked about. I was alone. There was no movement of dry leaf or loose stone. The ruins were, for the most part, open to the sky. Their rotting rafters had collapsed and joined together to form a low passage, like the entrance to a mine. This dark cavern seemed to lead down.

The smell was stronger when I approached this spot so I stopped again and waited there, wondering if I had discovered the lair of the leopard, wondering if the animal was now at rest after a night's hunt. Perhaps it was crouched there in the dark, watching me, recognizing me, knowing me as a man who walked alone in the forest without a weapon. I like to think that he was there and that he knew me and that he acknowledged my visit in the friendliest way—by ignoring me altogether.

Perhaps I had made him confident—too confident, too careless, too trusting of the human in his midst. I did not venture any further. I did not seek physical contact or even another glimpse of that beautiful sinewy body, springing from rock to rock... It was his trust I wanted and I think he gave it to me. But did the leopard, trusting one man, make the mistake of bestowing his trust on others? Did I, by casting out all fear—my own fear and the leopard's protective fear—leave him defenceless?

Because next day, coming up the path from the stream, shouting and beating their drums, were the shikaris. They had a long bamboo pole across their shoulder and slung from the pole, feet up, head down, was the lifeless body of the leopard. It had been shot in the neck and in the head.

'We told you there was a leopard!' they shouted, in great good humour. 'Isn't he a fine specimen?'

'Yes,' I said. 'He was a beautiful leopard.'

I walked home through the silent forest. It was very silent, almost as though the birds and animals knew their trust had been violated.

I remembered the lines of a poem by D.H. Lawrence and as I climbed the steep and lonely path to my home, the words beat out their rhythm in my mind—'There was room in the world for a mountain lion and me.'

EXCITING ENCOUNTERS

The following day, Mehmoud was making lamb chops. I liked lamb chops. Mehmoud knew I liked them, and he had an extra chop ready for me, just in case I felt like a pre-lunch snack.

'What was Jim Corbett's favourite dish?' I asked, while dealing with the succulent chop.

'Oh, he liked roast duck. Used to shoot them as they flew up from the *jheel*.'

'What's a jheel, Mehmoud?'

'A shallow sort of lake. In places you could walk about in the water. Different types of birds would come there in the winter—ducks and geese and all kinds of *bagla*s—herons, you call them. The baglas are not good to eat, but the ducks make a fine roast.

'So we camped beside the jheel and lived on roast duck for a week until everyone was sick of it.'

'Did you go swimming in the jheel?'

'No, it was full of muggers—those long-nosed crocodiles—they'll snap you up if you come within their range! Nasty creatures, those muggermuch. One of them nearly got me.'

'How did that happen, Mehmoud-bhai?'

'Oh, baba, just the memory of it makes me shudder! I'd given everyone their dinner and retired to my tent. It was a hot night and we couldn't sleep. Swarms of mosquitoes rose from the jheel, invaded the tent, and attacked me on the face and arms and feet. I dragged my camp cot outside the tent, hoping the breeze would keep the mosquitoes away. After some time they moved on, and I fell asleep, wrapped up in my bedsheet. Towards dawn, I felt my cot quivering, shaking. Was it an earthquake? But no one else was awake. And then the cot started moving! I sat up, looked about me. The cot was moving steadily forward in the direction of the water. And beneath it, holding us up, was a beastly crocodile!

'It gave me the fright of my life, baba. A muggermuch beneath my bed, and I upon it! I cried out for help. Carpet-sahib woke up, rushed out of his tent, his gun in his hands. But it was still dark, and all he could see was my bed moving rapidly towards the jheel.

'Just before we struck the water, I leapt from the cot, and ran up the bank, calling for help. Carpet-sahib saw me then. He ran down the slope, firing at the moving cot. I don't know if he hit the horrible creature, but there was a big splash, and it disappeared into the jheel.'

'And did you recover the cot?'

'No, it floated away and then sank. We did not go after it.'

'And what did Corbett say afterwards?'

'He said I had shown great presence of mind. He said he'd never seen anyone make such a leap for safety!'

'You were a hero, Mehmoud!'

'Thank you, baba. There's time for another lamb chop, if you're hungry.'

'I'm hungry,' I said. 'There's still an hour left to lunchtime. But tell me more about your time with Jim Corbett. Did he like your cooking?'

'Oh, *he* liked it well enough, but his sister was very fussy.'

'He had his sister with him?'

'That's right. He never married, so his sister looked after the household and the shopping and everything connected to the kitchen—except when we were in camp. Then I had a free hand. Carpet-sahib wasn't too fussy about his food, especially when he was out hunting. A sandwich or paratha would keep him going. But if he had guests, he felt he had to give them the best, and then it was hard work for me.

'For instance, there was the Raja of Janakpur, a big, fat man who was very fond of eating—between meals, during meals and after meals. I don't know why he bothered to come on these shikar trips when he could have stayed at home in his palace and feasted day and night. But he needed trophies to hang on the walls of his palace. You were not considered a great king unless your walls were decorated with the stuffed heads of tigers, lions, antelopes, bears—anything that looked dangerous. The Raja could eat and drink all day, but he couldn't go home without a trophy. So he would be hoisted onto an elephant, and sit there in state, firing away at anything that moved in the jungle. He seldom shot anything, but Carpet-sahib would help him out by bringing down a stag or a leopard, and congratulating the Raja on his skill and accuracy.

'They weren't all like that, but some of the Rajas were stupid or even mad. And the Angrej-sahibs—the English—were no better. They, too, had to prove their manliness by shooting a tiger or a leopard. Carpet-sahib was always in demand, because he lived at the edge of the jungle and knew where to look for different animals.

'The Raja of Janakpur was safe on an elephant, but one day he made the mistake of walking into the jungle on foot. He hadn't gone far when he met a wild boar running at him. A wild boar may not look very dangerous, but it has deadly tusks and is quick to use them. Before the Raja could raise the gun to his shoulder, the pig charged at him. The Raja dropped his gun, turned and ran for his life. But he couldn't run very fast or very far. He tripped and fell, and the boar was almost upon him when I happened along, looking for twigs to make a fire. Luckily, I had a small axe in my hand. I struck the boar over the head. It turned and rammed one of its tusks into my thigh. I struck at it again and again, till it fell dead at my feet. The Raja was nowhere in sight.

'As soon as he got into camp, he sent for his servants and made a hurried departure. Didn't even thank me for saving his life.'

'Were you hurt badly, Mehmoud?'

'I was out of action for a few days. The wound took time to heal. My new *masalchi* did all the cooking, and the food was so bad that most of the guests left in a hurry. I still have the scar. See, baba!'

Mehmoud drew up his pyjamas and showed me a deep scar on his right thigh.

'You were a hero, Mehmoud,' I said. 'You deserved a reward.'

'My reward is here, baba, preparing these lamb chops for you. Come on, have another. Your parents won't notice if they run short at lunch.'

TIGER, TIGER, BURNING BRIGHT

On the left bank of the Ganga, where it emerges from the Himalayan foothills, there is a long stretch of heavy forest. These are villages on the fringe of the forest, inhabited by bamboo cutters and farmers, but there are few signs of commerce or pilgrimage. Hunters, however, have found the area an ideal hunting ground during the last seventy years, and, as a result, the animals are not as numerous as they used to be. The trees, too, have been disappearing slowly; and, as the forest recedes, the animals lose their food and shelter and move on further into the foothills. Slowly, they are being denied the right to live.

Only the elephant can cross the river. And two years ago, when a large area of the forest was cleared to make way for a refugee resettlement camp, a herd of elephants—finding their favourite food, the green shoots of the bamboo, in short supply—waded across the river. They crashed through the suburbs of Haridwar, knocked down a factory wall, pulled down several tin roofs, held up a train, and left a trail of devastation in their wake until they found a new home in a new forest which was still untouched. Here, they settled down to a new life—but an unsettled, wary life. They did not know when men would appear again, with tractors, bulldozers, and dynamite.

There was a time when the forest on the banks of the Ganga had provided food and shelter for some thirty or forty tigers; but men in search of trophies had shot them all, and now there remained only one old tiger in the jungle. Many hunters had tried to get him, but he was a wise and crafty old tiger, who knew the ways of men, and he had so far survived all attempts on his life.

Although the tiger had passed the prime of his life, he had lost none of his majesty. His muscles rippled beneath the golden yellow of his coat, and he walked through the long grass with the confidence of one who knew that he was still a king, even though his subjects were fewer. His great head pushed through the foliage, and it was only his tail, swinging high, that showed occasionally above the sea of grass.

In late spring he would head for the large jheel, the only water in the forest (if you don't count the river, which was several miles away), which was almost a lake during the rainy season, but just a muddy marsh at this time of the year.

Here, at different times of the day and night, all the animals came to drink—the long-horned sambhar, the delicate chital, the swamp deer, the hyenas and jackals, the wild boar, the panthers—and the lone tiger. Since the elephants had gone, the water was usually clear except when buffaloes from the nearest village came to wallow in it, and then it was very muddy. These buffaloes, though they were not wild, were not afraid of the panther or even of the tiger. They knew the panther was afraid of their massive horns and that the tiger preferred the flesh of the deer.

One day, there were several sambhars at the water's edge; but they did not stay long. The scent of the tiger came with the breeze, and there was no mistaking its strong feline odour. The deer held their heads high for a few moments, their nostrils twitching, and then scattered into the forest, disappearing behind a screen of leaf and bamboo.

When the tiger arrived, there was no other animal near the water. But the birds were still there. The egrets continued to wade in the shallows, and a kingfisher darted low over the water, dived suddenly—a flash of blue and gold—and made off with a slim silver fish, which glistened in the sun like a polished gem. A long brown snake glided in and out among the waterlilies and disappeared beneath a fallen tree which lay rotting in the shallows.

The tiger waited in the shelter of a rock, his ears pricked up for the least unfamiliar sound; he knew that it was at that place that men sometimes sat up for him with guns, for they coveted his beauty—his stripes, and the gold of his body, his fine teeth, his whiskers and his noble head. They would have liked to hang his skin on a wall, with his head stuffed and mounted, and pieces of glass replacing his fierce eyes. Then they would have boasted of their triumph over the king of the jungle.

The tiger had encountered hunters before, so he did not usually show himself in the open during the day. But of late he had heard no guns, and if there were hunters around, you would have heard their guns (for a man with a gun cannot resist letting it off, even if it is only at a rabbit—or at another man). And, besides, the tiger was thirsty.

He was also feeling quite hot. It was March, and the shimmering dust haze of summer had come early. Tigers—unlike other cats—are fond of water, and on a hot day will wallow in it for hours.

He walked into the water, in amongst the waterlilies, and drank slowly. He was seldom in a hurry when he ate or drank. Other animals might bolt down their food, but they are only other animals. A tiger is a tiger; he has his dignity to preserve even though he isn't aware of it!

He raised his head and listened, one paw suspended in the air. A strange sound had come to him on the breeze, and he was wary of strange sounds. So he moved swiftly into the shelter of the tall grass that bordered the jheel, and climbed a hillock until he reached his favourite rock. This rock was big enough both to hide him and to give him shade. Anyone looking up from the jheel would have thought it strange that the rock had a round bump on the top. The bump was the tiger's head. He kept it very still.

The sound he heard was only the sound of a flute, rendered thin and reedy in the forest. It belonged to Ramu, a slim brown boy who rode a buffalo. Ramu played vigorously on the flute. Shyam, a slightly smaller boy, riding another buffalo, brought up the rear of the herd.

There were about eight buffaloes in the herd, and they belonged to the families of the two friends Ramu and Shyam. Their people were Gujars, a nomadic community who earned a livelihood by keeping buffaloes and selling milk and butter. The boys were about twelve years old, but they could not have told you exactly, because in their village nobody thought birthdays were important. They were almost the same age as the tiger, but he was old and experienced while they were still cubs.

The tiger had often seen them at the jheel, and he was not worried by their presence. He knew the village people would do him no harm as long as he left their buffaloes alone. Once, when he was younger and full of bravado, he had killed a buffalo—not because he was hungry, but because he was young and wanted to try out his strength—and after that the villagers had hunted him for days, with spears, bows and an old muzzleloader. Now he left the buffaloes alone, even though the deer in the forest were not as numerous as before.

The boys knew that a tiger lived in the jungle, for they had often heard him roar; but they did not suspect that he was so near just then.

The tiger gazed down from his rock, and the sight of eight fat black buffaloes made him give a low, throaty moan. But the boys were there. Besides, a buffalo was not easy to kill.

He decided to move on and find a cool shady place in the heart of the jungle where he could rest during the warm afternoon and be free of the flies and mosquitoes that swarmed around the jheel. At night he would hunt.

With a lazy, half-humorous roar—'*A-oonh*!'—he got up off his haunches and sauntered off into the jungle.

Even the gentlest of the tiger's roars can be heard half a mile away, and the boys, who were barely fifty yards away, looked up immediately.

'There he goes!' said Ramu, taking the flute from his lips and pointing it towards the hillocks. He was not afraid, for he knew that this tiger was not interested in humans. 'Did you see him?'

'I saw his tail, just before he disappeared. He's a big tiger!'

'Do not call him tiger. Call him uncle, or maharaja.'

'Oh, why?'

'Don't you know that it's unlucky to call a tiger a tiger? My father always told me so. If you meet a tiger, and call him uncle, he will leave you alone.'

'I'll try and remember that,' said Shyam.

The buffaloes were now well inside the water, and some of them were lying down in the mud. Buffaloes love soft wet mud and will wallow in it for hours. The slushier the mud the better. Ramu, to avoid being dragged down into the mud with his buffalo, slipped off its back and plunged into the water. He waded to a small islet covered with reeds and waterlilies. Shyam was close behind him.

They lay down on their hard flat stomachs, on a patch of grass, and allowed the warm sun to beat down on their bare brown bodies.

Ramu was the more knowledgeable boy because he had been to Hardiwar and Dehradun several times with his father. Shyam had never been out of the village.

Shyam said, 'The pool is not so deep this year.'

'We have had no rain since January,' said Ramu. 'If we do not get rain soon the jheel may dry up altogether.'

'And then what will we do?'

'We? I don't know. There is a well in the village. But even that may dry up. My father told me that it did once, just about the time I was born, and everyone had to walk ten miles to the river for water.'

'And what about the animals?'

'Some will stay here and die. Others will go to the river. But there are too many people near the river now—and temples, houses and factories—so the animals stay away. And the trees have been cut, so that between the jungle and the river there is no place to hide. Animals are afraid of the open—they are afraid of men with guns.'

'Even at night?'

'At night men come in jeeps, with searchlights. They kill the deer for meat, and sell the skins of tigers and panthers.'

'I didn't know a tiger's skin was worth anything.'

'It's worth more than our skins,' said Ramu knowingly. 'It will fetch six hundred rupees. Who would pay that much for one of us?'

'Our fathers would.'

'True—if they had the money.'

'If my father sold his fields, he would get more than six hundred rupees.'

'True—but if he sold his fields, none of you would have anything to eat. A man needs land as much as a tiger needs a jungle.'

'Yes,' said Shyam. 'And that reminds me—my mother asked me to take some roots home.'

'I will help you.'

They walked deeper into the jheel until the water was up to their waists, and began pulling up waterlilies by the roots. The flower is beautiful, but the villagers value the root more. When it is cooked, it makes a delicious and nourishing dish. The plant multiples rapidly and is aways in good supply. In the year when famine hit the village, it was only the root of the waterlily that saved many from starvation.

When Shyam and Ramu had finished gathering roots, they emerged from the water and passed the time wrestling with each other, slipping about in the soft mud, which soon covered them from head to toe.

To get rid of the mud, they dived into the water again and swam across to their buffaloes. Then, jumping on to their backs and digging their heels into the thick hides, the boys raced them across the jheel, shouting and hollering so much that all the birds flew away in fright, and the monkeys set up a shrill chattering of their own in the dhak trees. In March, the flame of the forest, or dhak trees, are ablaze with bright scarlet and orange flowers.

It was evening, and the twilight was fading fast, when the buffalo herd finally wandered its way homeward, to be greeted outside the village by the barking of dogs, the gurgle of hookah pipes, and the homely smell of cow-dung smoke.

The tiger made a kill that night—a chital. He made his approach against the wind so that the unsuspecting spotted deer did not see him until it was too late. A blow on the deer's haunches from the tiger's paw brought it down, and then the great beast fastened his fangs on the deer's throat. It was all over in a few minutes. The tiger was too quick and strong, and the deer did not struggle much.

It was a violent end for so gentle a creature. But you must not imagine that in the jungle the deer live in permanent fear of death. It is only man, with his imagination and his fear of the hereafter, who is afraid of dying. In the jungle it is different. Sudden death appears at intervals. Wild creatures do not have to think about it, and so the sudden killing of one of their number by some predator of the forest is only a fleeting incident soon forgotten by the survivors.

The tiger feasted well, growling with pleasure as he ate his way up the body, leaving the entrails. When he had had his night's fill, he left the carcass for the vultures and jackals. The cunning old tiger never returned to the same carcass, even if there was still plenty left to eat. In the past, when he had gone back to a kill, he had often found a man sitting in a tree waiting for him with a rifle.

His belly filled, the tiger sauntered over to the edge of the forest and looked out across the sandy wasteland and the deep, singing river, at the twinkling lights of Rishikesh on the opposite bank, and raised his head and roared his defiance at mankind.

He was a lonesome bachelor. It was five or six years since he had a mate. She had been shot by the trophy hunters, and her two cubs had been trapped by men who do trade in wild animals. One went to a circus, where he had to learn tricks to amuse men and respond to the crack of a whip; the other, more fortunate, went first to a zoo in Delhi and was later transferred to a zoo in America.

Sometimes, when the old tiger was very lonely, he gave a great roar, which could be heard throughout the forest. The villagers thought he was roaring in anger, but the jungle knew that he was really roaring out of loneliness. When the sound of his roar had died away, he paused, standing still, waiting for an answering roar; but it never came. It was taken up instead by the shrill scream of a barbet high up in a sal tree.

It was dawn now, dew-fresh and cool, and the jungle dwellers were on the move. The black beady little eyes of a jungle rat were fixed on a brown hen who was pecking around in the undergrowth near her nest. He had a large family to feed, this rat, and he knew that in the hen's nest was a clutch of delicious fawn-coloured eggs. He waited patiently for nearly an hour before he had the satisfaction of seeing the hen leave her nest and go off in search of food.

As soon as she had gone, the rat lost no time in making his raid. Slipping quietly out of his hole, he slithered along among the leaves; but, clever as he was, he did not realize that his own movements were being watched.

A pair of grey mongooses scouted about in the dry grass. They, too, were hungry, and eggs usually figured large on their menu. Now, lying still on an outcrop of rock, they watched the rat sneaking along, occasionally sniffing at the air and finally vanishing behind a boulder. When he reappeared, he was struggling to roll an egg uphill towards his hole.

The rat was in difficulty, pushing the egg sometimes with his paws, sometimes with his nose. The ground was rough, and the egg wouldn't move straight. Deciding that he must have help, he scuttled off to call his spouse. Even now the mongooses did not descend on the tantalizing egg. They waited until the rat returned with his wife, and then watched as the male rat took the egg firmly between his forepaws and rolled over on to his back. The female rat then grabbed her mate's tail and began to drag him along.

Totally absorbed in the struggle with the egg, the rat did not hear the approach of the mongooses. When these two large furry visitors suddenly bobbed up from behind a stone, the rats squealed with fright, abandoned the egg, and fled for their lives.

The mongooses wasted no time in breaking open the egg and making a meal of it. But just as, a few minutes ago, the rat had not noticed their approach, so now they did not notice the village boy, carrying a small bright axe and a net bag in his hands, creeping along.

Ramu, too, was searching for eggs, and when he saw the mongooses busy with one, he stood still to watch them, his eyes roving in search of the nest. He was hoping the mongooses would lead him to the nest; but, when they had finished their meal and made off into the undergrowth, Ramu had to do his own searching. He failed to find the nest, and moved further into the forest. The rat's hopes were just reviving when, to his disgust, the mother hen returned.

Ramu now made his way to a mahua tree.

The flowers of the mahua can be eaten by animals as well as by men. Bears are particularly fond of them and will eat large quantities of flowers, which gradually start fermenting in their stomachs with the result that the animals get quite drunk. Ramu had often seen a couple of bears stumbling home to their cave, bumping into each other or into the trunks of trees. They are short-sighted to begin with, and when drunk can hardly see at all. But their sense of smell and hearing are so good that in the end they find their way home.

Ramu decided he would gather some mahua flowers, and climbed up the tree, which is leafless when it blossoms. He began breaking the white flowers and throwing them to the ground. He had been on the tree for about five minutes when he heard the whining grumble of a bear, and presently a young sloth bear ambled into the clearing beneath the tree.

He was a small bear, little more than a cub, and Ramu was

not frightened; but, because he thought the mother might be in the vicinity, he decided to take no chances, and sat very still, waiting to see what the bear would do. He hoped it wouldn't choose the mahua tree for a meal.

At first, the young bear put his nose to the ground and sniffed his way along until he came to a large anthill. Here he began huffing and puffing, blowing rapidly in and out of his nostrils, causing the dust from the anthill to fly in all directions. But he was a disappointed bear, because the anthill had been deserted long ago. And so, grumbling, he made his way across to a tall wild plum tree, and shinning rapidly up the smooth trunk, was soon perched on its topmost branches. It was only then that he saw Ramu.

The bear at once scrambled several feet higher up the tree, and laid himself out flat on a branch. It wasn't a very thick branch and left a large expanse of bear showing on either side. The bear tucked his head away behind another branch, and so long as he could not see Ramu, seemed quite satisfied that he was well hidden, though he couldn't help grumbling with anxiety, for a bear, like most animals, is afraid of man.

Bears, however, are also very curious—and curiosity has often led them into trouble. Slowly, inch by inch, the young bear's black snout appeared over the edge of the branch; but as soon as the eyes came into view and met Ramu's, he drew back with a jerk and the head was once more hidden. The bear did this two or three times, and Ramu, highly amused, waited until it wasn't looking, then moved some way down the tree. When the bear looked up again and saw that the boy was missing, he was so pleased with himself that he stretched right across to the next branch, to get a plum. Ramu chose this moment to burst into loud laughter. The startled bear tumbled out of the tree, dropped through the branches for a distance of some fifteen feet, and landed with a thud in a heap of dry leaves.

And then several things happened at almost the same time.

The mother bear came charging into the clearing. Spotting Ramu in the tree, she reared up on her hind legs, grunting fiercely. It was Ramu's turn to be startled. There are few animals more dangerous than a rampaging mother bear, and the boy knew that one blow from her clawed forepaws could rip his skull open.

But before the bear could approach the tree, there was a tremendous roar, and the old tiger bounded into the clearing. He had been asleep in the bushes not far away—he liked a good sleep after a heavy meal—and the noise in the clearing had woken him.

He was in a bad mood, and his loud *'A-oonh!'* made his displeasure quite clear. The bears turned and ran from the clearing, the youngster squealing with fright.

The tiger then came into the centre of the clearing, looked up at the trembling boy, and roared again.

Ramu nearly fell out of the tree.

'Good day to you, Uncle,' he stammered, showing his teeth in a nervous grin.

Perhaps this was too much for the tiger. With a low growl, he turned his back on the mahua tree and padded off into the jungle, his tail twitching in disgust.

That night, when Ramu told his parents and his grandfather about the tiger and how he had saved him from a female bear, it started a round of tiger stories—about how some of them could be gentlemen, others rogues. Sooner or later the conversation came round to man-eaters, and Grandfather told two stories which he swore were true, although his listeners only half believed him.

The first story concerned the belief that a man-eating tiger is guided towards his next victim by the spirit of a human being previously killed and eaten by the tiger. Grandfather said that he actually knew three hunters who sat up in a *machan* over a human kill, and when the tiger came, the corpse sat up and pointed with his right hand at the men in the tree. The tiger then went away. But the hunters knew he would return, and one man was brave enough to get down from the tree and tie the right arm of the corpse to its side. Later, when the tiger returned, the corpse sat up and this time pointed out the men with his left hand. The enraged tiger sprang into the tree and killed his enemies in the machan.

'And then there was a bania,' said Grandfather, beginning another story, 'who lived in a village in the jungle. He wanted to visit a neighbouring village to collect some money that was owed to him, but as the road lay through heavy forest in which lived a terrible man-eating tiger, he did not know what to do. Finally, he went to a sadhu, who gave him two powders. By eating the first powder he could turn into a huge tiger, capable of dealing with any other tiger in the jungle, and by eating the second he would become a bania again.

'Armed with his two powders, and accompanied by his pretty, young wife, the bania set out on his journey. They had not gone far into the forest when they came upon the man-eater sitting in the middle of the road. Before swallowing the first powder, the bania told his wife to stay where she was, so that when he returned after killing the tiger, she could at once give him the second powder and enable him to resume his old shape.

'Well, the bania's plan worked, but only up to a point. He swallowed the first powder and immediately became a magnificent tiger. With a great roar, he bounded towards the man-eater, and after a brief, furious fight, killed his opponent. Then, with his jaws still dripping blood, he returned to his wife.

'The poor girl was terrified and spilt the second powder on the ground. The bania was so angry that he pounced on his wife and killed and ate her. And afterwards, this terrible tiger was so enraged at not being able to become a human again that he killed and ate hundreds of people all over the country.'

'The only people he spared,' added Grandfather, with a twinkle in his eyes, 'were those who owed him money. A bania never gives up a loan as lost, and the tiger still hoped that one day he might become a human again and be able to collect his dues.'

Next morning, when Ramu came back from the well which was used to irrigate his father's fields, he found a crowd of curious children surrounding a jeep and three strangers with guns. Each of the strangers had a gun, and they were accompanied by two bearers and a vast amount of provisions.

They had heard that there was a tiger in the area, and they wanted to shoot it.

One of the hunters, who looked even more strange than the others, had come all the way from America to shoot a tiger, and he vowed that he would not leave the country without a tiger's skin in his baggage. One of his companions had said that he could buy a tiger's skin in Delhi, but the hunter said he preferred to get his own trophies.

These men had money to spend, and as most of the villagers needed money badly, they were only too willing to go into the forest to construct a machan for the hunters. The platform, big enough to take the three men, was put up in the branches of a tall toon, or mahogany, tree.

It was the only night the hunters used the machan. At the end of March, though the days are warm, the nights are still cold.

The hunters had neglected to bring blankets, and by midnight, their teeth were chattering. Ramu, having tied up a buffalo calf for them at the foot of the tree, made as if to go home but instead circled the area, hanging up bits and pieces of old clothing on small trees and bushes. He thought he owed that much to the tiger. He knew the wily old king of the jungle would keep well away from the bait if he saw the bits of clothing—for where there were men's clothes, there would be men.

The vigil lasted well into the night but the tiger did not come near the toon tree. Perhaps he wasn't hungry; perhaps he got Ramu's message. In any case, the men in the tree soon gave themselves away.

The cold was really too much for them. A flask of rum was produced, and passed round, and it was not long before there was more purpose to finishing the rum than to finishing off a tiger. Silent at first, the men soon began talking in whispers; and to jungle creatures a human whisper is as telling as a trumpet call.

Soon the men were quite merry, talking in loud voices. And when the first morning light crept over the forest, and Ramu and his friends came back to fetch the great hunters, they found them fast asleep in the machan.

The hunters looked surly and embarrassed as they trudged back to the village.

'No game left in these parts,' said the American.

'Wrong time of the year for tiger,' said the second man.

'Don't know what the country's coming to,' said the third.

And complaining about the weather, the poor quality of cartridges, the quantity of rum they had drunk, and the perversity of tigers, they drove away in disgust.

It was not until the onset of summer that an event occurred which altered the hunting habits of the old tiger and brought him into conflict with the villagers.

There had been no rain for almost two months, and the tall jungle grass had become a sea of billowy dry yellow. Some refugee settlers, living in an area where the forest had been cleared, had been careless while cooking and had started a jungle fire. Slowly it spread into the interior, from where the acrid smell and the fumes smoked the tiger out towards the edge of the jungle. As night came on, the flames grew more vivid, and the smell stronger. The tiger turned and made for the jheel, where he knew he would be safe provided he swam across to the little island in the centre.

Next morning he was on the island, which was untouched by the fire. But his surroundings had changed. The slopes of the hills were black with burnt grass, and most of the tall bamboo had disappeared. The deer and the wild pig, finding that their natural cover had gone, fled further east.

When the fire had died down and the smoke had cleared, the tiger prowled through the forest again but found no game. Once he came across the body of a burnt rabbit, but he could not eat it. He drank at the jheel and settled down in a shady spot to sleep the day away. Perhaps, by evening, some of the animals would return. If not, he, too, would have to look for new hunting grounds—or new game.

The tiger spent five more days looking for suitable game to kill. By that time he was so hungry that he even resorted to rooting among the dead leaves and burnt out stumps of trees, searching for worms and beetles. This was a sad comedown for the king of the jungle. But even now he hesitated to leave the area, for he had a deep suspicion and fear of the forest further east—forests that were fast being swallowed up by human habitation. He could have gone north, into high mountains, but they did not provide him with the long grass he needed. A panther could manage quite well up there, but not a tiger, who loved the natural privacy of the heavy jungle. In the hills, he would have to hide all the time.

At break of day, the tiger came to the jheel. The water was now shallow and muddy, and a green scum had spread over the top. But it was still drinkable and the tiger quenched his thirst.

He lay down across his favourite rock, hoping for a deer but none came. He was about to get up and go away when he heard an animal approach.

The tiger at once leaped off his perch and flattened himself on the ground, his tawny striped skin merging with the dry grass. A heavy animal was moving through the bushes, and the tiger waited patiently.

A buffalo emerged and came to the water.

The buffalo was alone.

He was a big male, and his long curved horns lay right back across his shoulders. He moved leisurely towards the water, completely unaware of the tiger's presence.

The tiger hesitated before making his charge. It was a long time—many years—since he had killed a buffalo, and he knew the villagers would not like it. But the pangs of hunger overcame his scruples. There was no morning breeze, everything was still, and the smell of the tiger did not reach the buffalo. A monkey chattered on a nearby tree, but his warning went unheeded.

Crawling stealthily on his stomach, the tiger skirted the edge of the jheel and approached the buffalo from the rear. The waterbirds, who were used to the presence of both animals, did not raise an alarm.

Getting closer, the tiger glanced around to see if there were men, or other buffaloes, in the vicinity. Then, satisfied that he was alone, he crept forward. The buffalo was drinking, standing in shallow water at the edge of the jheel, when the tiger charged from the side and bit deep into the animal's thigh.

The buffalo turned to fight, but the tendons of his right hind leg had been snapped, and he could only stagger forward a few paces. But he was a buffalo—the bravest of the domestic cattle. He was not afraid. He snorted, and lowered his horns at the tiger; but the great cat was too fast, and circling the buffalo, bit into the other hind leg.

The buffalo crashed to the ground, both hind legs crippled, and then the tiger dashed in, using both tooth and claw, biting deep into the buffalo's throat until the blood gushed out from the jugular vein.

The buffalo gave one long, last bellow before dying.

The tiger, having rested, now began to gorge himself, but, even though he had been starving for days, he could not finish the huge carcass. At least one good meal still remained when, satisfied and feeling his strength returning, he quenched his thirst at the jheel. Then he dragged the remains of the buffalo into the bushes to hide it from the vultures, and went off to find a place to sleep.

He would return to the kill when he was hungry.

The villagers were upset when they discovered that a buffalo was missing; and the next day, when Ramu and Shyam came running home to say that they had found the carcass near the jheel, half eaten by a tiger, the men were disturbed and angry. They felt that the tiger had tricked and deceived them. And they knew that once he got a taste for domestic cattle, he would make a habit of slaughtering them.

Kundan Singh, Shyam's father and the owner of the dead buffalo, said he would go after the tiger himself.

'It is all very well to talk about what you will do to the tiger,' said his wife, 'but you should never have let the buffalo go off on its own.'

'He had been out on his own before,' said Kundan. 'This is

the first time the tiger has attacked one of our beasts. A devil must have entered the maharaja.'

'He must have been very hungry,' said Shyam.

'Well, we are hungry too,' said Kundan Singh.

'Our best buffalo—the only male in our herd.'

'The tiger will kill again,' said Ramu's father.

'If we let him,' said Kundan.

'Should we send for the shikaris?'

'No. They were not clever. The tiger will escape them easily. Besides, there is no time. The tiger will return for another meal tonight. We must finish him off ourselves!'

'But how?'

Kundan Singh smiled secretively, played with the ends of his moustache for a few moments, and then, with great pride, produced from under his cot a double-barrelled gun of ancient vintage.

'My father bought it from an Englishman,' he said.

'How long ago was that?'

'At the time I was born.'

'And have you ever used it?' asked Ramu's father, who was not sure that the gun would work.

'Well, some years back I let it off at some bandits. You remember the time when those dacoits raided our village? They chose the wrong village, and were severely beaten for their pains. As they left, I fired my gun off at them. They didn't stop running until they crossed the Ganga!'

'Yes, but did you hit anyone?'

'I would have, if someone's goat hadn't got in the way at the last moment. But we had roast mutton that night! Don't worry, brother, I know how the thing fires.'

Accompanied by Ramu's father and some others, Kundan Singh set out for the jheel, where, without shifting the buffalo's carcass—for they knew that the tiger would not come near them if he suspected a trap—they made another machan in the branches of a tall tree some thirty feet from the kill.

Later that evening, Kundan Singh and Ramu's father settled down for the night on their crude platform in the tree.

Several hours passed, and nothing but a jackal was seen by the watchers. And then, just as the moon came up over the distant hills, Kundan and his companion were startled by a low '*A-oonh!*', followed by a suppressed, rumbling growl.

Kundan grasped his old gun, whilst his friend drew closer to him for comfort. There was complete silence for a minute or two—time that was an agony of suspense for the watchers—and then the sound of stealthy footfalls on dead leaves under the trees.

A moment later, the tiger walked out into the moonlight and stood over his kill.

At first Kundan could do nothing. He was completely overawed by the size of this magnificent tiger. Ramu's father had to nudge him, and then Kundan quickly put the gun to his shoulder, aimed at the tiger's head, and pressed the trigger.

The gun went off with a flash and two loud bangs, as Kundan fired both barrels. Then there was a tremendous roar. One of the bullets had grazed the tiger's head.

The enraged animal rushed at the tree and tried to leap up into the branches. Fortunately, the machan had been built at a safe height, and the tiger was unable to reach it. He roared again and then bounded off into the forest.

'What a tiger!' exclaimed Kundan, half in fear and half in admiration. 'I feel as though my liver has turned to water.'

'You missed him completely,' said Ramu's father. 'Your gun makes a big noise; an arrow would have done more damage.'

'I did not miss him,' said Kundan, feeling offended. 'You heard him roar, didn't you? Would he have been so angry if he had not been hit? If I have wounded him badly, he will die.'

'And if you have wounded him slightly, he may turn into a man-eater, and then where will we be?'

'I don't think he will come back,' said Kundan. 'He will leave these forests.'

They waited until the sun was up before coming down from the tree. They found a few drops of blood on the dry grass but no trail led into the forest, and Ramu's father was convinced that the wound was only a slight one.

The bullet, missing the fatal spot behind the ear, had only grazed the back of the skull and cut a deep groove at its base. It took a few days to heal, and during this time the tiger lay low and did not go near the jheel except when it was very dark and he was very thirsty.

The villagers thought the tiger had gone away, and Ramu and Shyam—accompanied by some other youths, and always carrying axes and lathis—began bringing buffaloes to the jheel again during the day; but they were careful not to let any of them stray far from the herd, and they returned home while it was still daylight.

It was some days since the jungle had been ravaged by the fire, and in the tropics the damage is repaired quickly. In spite of it being the dry season, new life was creeping into the forest.

While the buffaloes wallowed in the muddy water, and the boys wrestled on the grassy island, a big tawny eagle soared high above them, looking for a meal—a sure sign that some of the animals were beginning to return to the forest. It was not long before his keen eyes detected a movement in the glade below.

What the eagle with his powerful eyesight saw was a baby hare, a small fluffy thing, its long pink-tinted ears laid flat along its sides. Had it not been creeping along between two large stones, it would have escaped notice. The eagle waited to see if the mother was about, and as he waited he realized that he was not the only one who coveted this juicy morsel. From the bushes there had appeared a sinuous yellow creature, pressed, low to the ground and moving rapidly towards the hare. It was a yellow jungle cat, hardly noticeable in the scorched grass. With great stealth the jungle cat began to stalk the baby hare.

He pounced. The hare's squeal was cut short by the cat's cruel claws; but it had been heard by the mother hare, who now bounded into the glade and without the slightest hesitation went for the surprised cat.

There was nothing haphazard about the mother hare's attack. She flashed around behind the cat and jumped clean over him. As she landed, she kicked back, sending a stinging jet of dust shooting into the cat's face. She did this again and again.

The bewildered cat, crouching and snarling, picked up the kill and tried to run away with it. But the hare would not permit this. She continued her leaping and buffeting, till eventually the cat, out of sheer frustration, dropped the kill and attacked the mother.

The cat sprang at the hare a score of times, lashing out with his claws; but the mother hare was both clever and agile enough to keep just out of reach of those terrible claws, and drew the cat further and further away from her baby—for she did not as yet know that it was dead.

The tawny eagle saw his chance. Swift and true, he swooped. For a brief moment, as his wings overspread the furry small little hare and his talons sank deep into it, he caught a glimpse of the cat racing towards him and the mother hare fleeing into the bushes. And then with a shrill '*kee-ee-ee*' of triumph, he rose and whirled away with his dinner.

The boys had heard his shrill cry and looked up just in time to see the eagle flying over the jheel with the little hare held firmly in his talons.

'Poor hare,' said Shyam. 'Its life was short.'

'That's the law of the jungle,' said Ramu. 'The eagle has a family, too, and must feed it.'

'I wonder if we are any better than animals,' said Shyam.

'Perhaps we are a little better, in some ways,' said Ramu. 'Grandfather always says, "To be able to laugh and to be merciful are the only things that make man better than the beast."'

The next day, while the boys were taking the herd home, one of the buffaloes lagged behind. Ramu did not realize that the animal was missing until he heard an agonized bellow behind him. He glanced over his shoulder just in time to see the big striped tiger dragging the buffalo into a clump of young bamboo. At the same time, the herd became aware of the danger, and the buffaloes snorted with fear as they hurried along the forest path. To urge them forward, and to warn his friends, Ramu cupped his hands to his mouth and gave vent to a yodelling call.

The buffaloes bellowed, the boys shouted, and the birds flew shrieking from the trees. It was almost a stampede by the time the herd emerged from the forest. The villagers heard the thunder of hoofs, and saw the herd coming home amidst clouds of dust and confusion, and knew that something was wrong.

'The tiger!' shouted Ramu. 'He is here! He has killed one of the buffaloes.'

'He is afraid of us no longer,' said Shyam.

'Did you see where he went?' asked Kundan Singh, hurrying up to them.

'I remember the place,' said Ramu. 'He dragged the buffalo in amongst the bamboo.'

'Then there is no time to lose,' said his father. 'Kundan, you take your gun and two men, and wait near the suspension bridge, where the Garur stream joins the Ganga. The jungle is narrow there. We will beat the jungle from our side, and drive the tiger towards you. He will not escape us, unless he swims the river!'

'Good!' said Kundan Singh, running into his house for his gun, with Shyam close at his heels. 'Was it one of our buffaloes again?' he asked.

'It was Ramu's buffalo this time,' said Shyam. 'A good milk buffalo.'

'Then Ramu's father will beat the jungle thoroughly. You boys had better come with me. It will not be safe for you to accompany the beaters.'

Kundan Singh, carrying his gun and accompanied by Ramu, Shyam and two men, headed for the river junction, while Ramu's father collected about twenty men from the village and, guided by one of the boys who had been with Ramu, made for the spot where the tiger had killed the buffalo.

The tiger was still eating when he heard the men coming. He had not expected to be disturbed so soon. With an angry 'Whoof!' he bounded into a bamboo thicket and watched the men through a screen of leaves and tall grass.

The men did not seem to take much notice of the dead buffalo, but gathered round their leader and held a consultation. Most of them carried hand drums slung from their shoulders. They also carried sticks, spears and axes.

After a hurried conversation, they entered the denser part of the jungle, beating their drums with the palms of their hands. Some of the men banged empty kerosene tins. These made even more noise than the drums.

The tiger did not like the noise and retreated deeper into the jungle. But he was surprised to find that the men, instead of going away, came after him into the jungle, banging away on their drums and tins, and shouting at the top of their voices.

They had separated now, and advanced single or in pairs, but nowhere were they more than fifteen yards apart. The tiger could easily have broken through this slowly advancing semicircle of men—one swift blow from his paw would have felled the strongest of them—but his main aim was to get away from the noise. He hated and feared noise made by men.

He was not a man-eater and he would not attack a man unless he was very angry or frightened or very desperate; and he was none of these things as yet. He had eaten well, and he would have liked to rest in peace—but there would be no rest for any animal until the men ceased their tremendous clatter and din.

For an hour Ramu's father and the others beat the jungle, calling, drumming and trampling the undergrowth. The tiger had no rest. Whenever he was able to put some distance between himself and the men, he would sink down in some shady spot to rest; but, within five or ten minutes, the trampling and drumming would sound nearer, and the tiger, with an angry snarl, would get up and pad north, pad silently north along the narrowing strip of jungle, towards the junction of the Garur stream and the Ganga. Ten years ago, he would have had the jungle on his right in which to hide; but the trees had been felled long ago to make way for humans and houses, and now he could only move to the left, towards the river.

It was about noon when the tiger finally appeared in the open. He longed for the darkness and security of the night, for the sun was his enemy. Kundan and the boys had a clear view of him as he stalked slowly along—now in the open with the sun glinting on his glossy hide, now in the shade or passing through the shorter reeds. He was still out of range of Kundan's gun, but there was no fear of his getting out of the beat, as the 'stops' were all picked men from the village. He disappeared among some bushes but soon reappeared to retrace his steps, the beaters having done their work well. He was now only one hundred and fifty yards from the rocks where Kundan Singh waited, and he looked very big.

The beat had closed in, and the exit along the bank downstream was completely blocked, so the tiger turned and disappeared into a belt of reeds, and Kundan Singh expected that the head would soon peer out of the cover a few yards away. The beaters were now making a great noise, shouting and beating their drums, but nothing moved; and Ramu, watching from a distance, wondered, 'Has he slipped through the beaters?' And he half hoped so.

Tins clashed, drums beat, and some of the men poked into the reeds with their spears or long bamboos. Perhaps one of these thrusts found a mark, because at last the tiger was roused, and with an angry desperate snarl, he charged out of the reeds, splashing his way through an inlet of mud and water. Kundan Singh fired, and his bullet struck the tiger on the thigh.

The mighty animal stumbled; but he was up in a minute, and rushing through a gap in the narrowing line of beaters, he made straight for the only way across the river—the suspension bridge that passed over the Ganga here, providing a route into the high hills beyond.

'We'll get him now,' said Kundan, priming his gun again. 'He's right in the open!'

The suspension bridge swayed and trembled as the wounded tiger lurched across it. Kundan fired, and this time the bullet grazed the tiger's shoulder. The animal bounded forward, lost his footing on the unfamiliar, slippery planks of the swaying bridge, and went over the side, falling headlong into the strong, swirling waters of the river.

He rose to the surface once, but the current took him

under and away, and only a thin streak of blood remained on the river's surface.

Kundan and others hurried downstream to see if the dead tiger had been washed up on the river's banks; but though they searched the riverside for several miles, they did not find the king of the forest.

He had not provided anyone with a trophy. His skin would not be spread on a couch, nor would his head be hung up on a wall. No claw of his would be hung as a charm round the neck of a child. No villager would use his fat as a cure for rheumatism.

At first the villagers were glad because they felt their buffaloes were safe. Then the men began to feel that something had gone out of their lives, out of the life of the forest; they began to feel that the forest was no longer a forest. It had been shrinking year by year, but, as long as the tiger had been there and the villagers had heard it roar at night, they had known that they were still secure from the intruders and newcomers who came to fell the trees and eat up the land and let the flood waters into the village. But now that the tiger had gone, it was as though a protector had gone, leaving the forest open and vulnerable, easily destroyable. And once the forest was destroyed they, too, would be in danger…

There was another thing that had gone with the tiger, another thing that had been lost, a thing that was being lost everywhere—something called 'nobility'.

Ramu remembered something that his grandfather had once said. 'The tiger is the very soul of India, and when the last tiger goes, so will the soul of the country.'

The boys lay flat on their stomachs on their little mud island and watched the monsoon clouds gathering overhead.

'The king of our forest is dead,' said Shyam. 'There are no more tigers.'

'There must be tigers,' said Ramu. 'How can there be an India without tigers?'

The river had carried the tiger many miles away from his home, from the forest he had always known, and brought him ashore on a strip of warm yellow sand, where he lay in the sun, quite still, but breathing.

Vultures gathered and waited at a distance, some of them perching on the branches of nearby trees.

But the tiger was more drowned than hurt, and as the river water oozed out of his mouth, and the warm sun made new life throb through his body, he stirred and stretched, and his glazed eyes came into focus. Raising his head, he saw trees and tall grass.

Slowly, he heaved himself off the ground and moved at a crouch to where the grass waved in the afternoon breeze. Would he be harried again, and shot at? There was no smell of man. The tiger moved forward with greater confidence.

There was, however, another smell in the air—a smell that reached back to the time when he was young and fresh and full of vigour—a smell that he had almost forgotten but could never quite forget: the smell of a tigress!

He raised his head high, and new life surged through his tired limbs. He gave a full-throated roar and moved purposefully through the tall grass. And the roar came back to him, calling him, calling him forward: a roar that meant there would be more tigers in the land!

MONKEYS IN THE LOO

I am fairly tolerant about these monkeys doing the bhangra on my roof, but I do resent it when they start invading my rooms. Not so long ago, I opened the bathroom door to find a very large Rhesus monkey sitting on the potty. He wasn't actually using the potty—monkeys prefer parapet walls—but he had obviously found it a comfortable place to sit, and he showed no signs of vacating the throne when politely requested to do so. Bullies seldom do. So I had to give him a fright by slamming the door as loudly as I could, and he took off through the open window and found his cousins on the hillside.

On another occasion, a female of the species sat on my desk, lifted the telephone receiver and appeared to be making an STD call to some distant relative. Some ladies are apt to linger long over their calls, and I hated to interrupt, but I was anxious to get in touch with my publisher, who took priority; so I pushed her off my desk with a feather-duster. She was so resentful of this intrusion that she made off with my telephone directory and tore it to shreds, scattering pages along the road. As this was something that I had wanted to do for a long time, I could not help admiring her audacity.

The kitchen area of our flat is closely guarded, as I resent sharing my breakfast with creatures great and small. But the other day a wily crow flew in and made off with my boiled egg. I know crows are fond of eggs—other birds' eggs that is—but I did not know that they like them boiled. Anyway, this egg was still piping hot, and the crow had to drop it on the road, where it was seized upon by one of the stray dogs who police this end of the road.

Barking furiously, the dogs run after the monkeys, who simply leap onto the nearest tree or rooftop and proceed to throw insults at the frustrated pack. The dogs never succeed in catching anything except their own kind. Canine intruders from another area are readily attacked and driven away.

♦

Having dressed, breakfasted and written the morning's two or three pages (early morning is the best time to do this), I am free to walk up the road to the bank or post office or tea shop at the top of the hill. If it's springtime, I shall look out for wild flowers. If it's monsoon time; I shall look out for leeches.

Well, it's monsoon time, and we haven't seen the sun for a couple of weeks. Clouds envelop the hills, and a light shower is falling. I have unfurled my bright yellow umbrella, as a gesture of defiance. At least it provides some contrast to the grey sky and the dark green of the hillside. You cannot see the snows or even the next mountain.

There's no one else on the road today, only a few intrepid tourists from Amritsar. I overhead one robust Punjabi complain to his guide: 'You've brought us all the way to the top of this forsaken mountain, and what have you shown us? The *kabristan*!'

True, the old British graves are all that one can see through the fog. Some of the tombstones have been standing there for close on two centuries. The old abandoned parsonage next door to the cemetery is now the home of Victor Banerjee, the celebrated actor. He enjoys living next door to the graveyard, and one night he defied me to walk home alone past the graves. I am not a superstitious person but I did feel rather uneasy as those old graves loomed up through the mist. I was startled by the cry of a night-bird emanating from behind one of the tombstones. Then a weird, blood-chilling cry rose from a clump of bushes. It was Victor, trying to frighten me—or possibly practising for his next role as Dracula. I was about to break into a run when a large dog—one of our strays—appeared beside me and accompanied me home. On a dark and scary night, even a half-starved mongrel is welcome company. By day, the road holds no terrors. But there are other hazards. On the road near Char Dukan, several small boys are kicking a football around. The ball rolls temptingly towards me. Remembering my football skills of fifty or more years ago, I cannot resist the temptation to put boot to ball. I give it a mighty kick. The ball sails away, the children applaud, I am left hopping about on the road in agony, I had quite forgotten my gout! I'm glad I stuck to writing instead of taking up professional football. At seventy I can still write without inflicting damage on myself.

◆

When I am feeling good, and have the road to myself, I do occasionally break into song. This is the only opportunity I have to sing. Otherwise my musical abilities turn friends into foes.

I am not permitted to sing in the homes of my friends. If I am being driven about in their cars, I am told to remain silent unless we veer off the road or hit an oncoming vehicle. Even at home, the sound of my music causes the girls to drop dishes and the children to find an excuse to stop doing their homework.

'Dada is ill again,' says Gautam, when all I am trying to do is emulate Caruso singing 'Che Gelida Nlanina' (Your Tiny Hand is Frozen) from *La Boheme*. Our tiny hands do freeze up here in the winter, and there's nothing like an operatic aria to get the blood circulating freely. Of course Caruso was a tenor, but I can also sing baritone like Domingo or Nelson Eddy and bass like Chaliapin, the great Russian singer. Sometimes

I combine all three voices—tenor, baritone, bass—and that's when the window glass shatters and cars come to a screeching halt.

It was a boyhood ambition to be an opera star, but I'm afraid I never made it beyond the school choir. Our music teacher did not appreciate the wide range of my voice. 'Too loud!' she would screech. 'Too flat!'

'Caruso sings in A-flat,' I replied.

'You sound like a warbling frog,' she snapped. 'And you look like one,' I responded.

And that was the end of my brief appearance in cassock and surplice.

But when I'm on the open road—especially when it's raining and I have the road to myself—I am free to sing as loud and as flat as I like, and if flat tyres on passing cars are the result, it's the fault of the tyres and not my singing.

So here we go:

When you are down and out,
Lift up your head and shout—
It's going to be a great day!

There's nothing like a spirited song to raise the flagging spirit. Whenever I feel down and out—and that's often enough—I recall some old favourite and share it with the trees, the birds, and even those pesky monkeys.

Just like a sunflower
After a summer shower
My inspiration is you!

Sloppy, sentimental stuff, but it works.

And there's always the likelihood of a little romance around the corner.

Some enchanted evening
You will see a stranger
Across a crowded room...

Actually, I prefer the winding road to a crowded room. Romantic encounters are more likely when there are not too many people around. Such as the other day, when I had unfurled my new umbrella and was sauntering up the road, singing my favourite rain song, Sinking in the Rain.

I had gone some distance when I noticed a young lady struggling up the road a little way ahead of me. My glasses were wet and misty, but I was determined to share my umbrella with any damsel in distress. So, huffing and puffing, I caught up with her.

'Do share my umbrella,' I offered.

No, she wasn't sweet twenty-one, as I'd hoped. She was nearer eighty. But she was munching on a *bhutta*, so her teeth were in good order. She took the umbrella from me and munched on ahead, leaving me to get drenched. A retired headmistress, as I discovered later!

She returned the umbrella when we got to Char Dukan, but in future I shall make a frontal approach before making any gallant overtures on the road. Those crowded rooms are safer.

Monsoon time, and umbrellas are taken out and frequently lost. I lost three last year. One was borrowed, and as you know, borrowed books and umbrellas are seldom returned. By some mysterious process they become the permanent property of the borrower. Another disappeared while I was cashing a cheque in the bank. And the third was wrecked in the following fashion.

Coming down from Char Dukan, I found two hefty boys engaged in furious combat in the middle of the road. One was a kick-boxer, the other a kung-fu exponent. Afraid that one of them would be badly hurt, I decided to intervene, and called out, 'Come on boys, break it up!' I thrust my umbrella between them in a bid to end the fracas. My umbrella received a mighty kick, and went sailing across the road and over the parapet. The boys stopped fighting in order to laugh at my discomfiture. One of them retrieved my umbrella, minus its handle.

In a way, I'd been successful as a peacemaker—certainly more successful than the United Nations—although at some cost to my personal property. Well, we peacemakers must be prepared to put up with a little inconvenience.

I'm a great believer in the Law of Compensation (as propounded by Emerson in his famous essay)—that what we do, good or bad, is returned in full measure in this life rather than in the hereafter.

Not long after the incident just described, there was my old friend Vipin Buckshey standing on the threshold with a seasonal gift—a beautiful blue umbrella!

He did not know about the street-fighter, but had read my story 'The Blue Umbrella'—a simple tale about greed being overcome by generosity—and had bought me a blue umbrella in appreciation. I shall be careful not to lose it.

GRANDPA FIGHTS AN OSTRICH

Before my grandfather joined the Indian Railways, he worked for a few years on the East African Railways, and it was during that period that he had his now famous encounter with the ostrich. My childhood was frequently enlivened by this oft-told tale of his, and I give it here in his own words—or as well as I can remember them!

While engaged in the laying of a new railway line, I had a miraculous escape from an awful death. I lived in a small township, but my work lay some twelve miles away, and I had to go to the work site and back on horseback.

One day, my horse had a slight accident, so I decided to do the journey on foot, being a great walker in those days. I also knew of a short cut through the hills that would save me about six miles.

This short cut went through an ostrich farm—or 'camp', as it was called. It was the breeding season. I was fairly familiar with the ways of ostriches, and knew that male birds were very aggressive in the breeding season, ready to attack on the slightest provocation, but I also knew that my dog would scare away any bird that might try to attack me. Strange though it may seem, even the biggest ostrich (and some of them grow to a height of nine feet) will run faster than a racehorse at the sight of even a small dog. So, I felt quite safe in the company of my dog, a mongrel who had adopted me some two months previously.

On arrival at the 'camp', I climbed through the wire fencing and, keeping a good look out, dodged across the open spaces between the thorn bushes. Now and then I caught a glimpse of the birds feeding some distance away.

I had gone about half a mile from the fencing when up started a hare. In an instant my dog gave chase. I tried calling him back, even though I knew it was hopeless. Chasing hares was that dog's passion.

I don't know whether it was the dog's bark or my own shouting, but what I was most anxious to avoid immediately happened. The ostriches were startled and began darting to and fro. Suddenly, I saw a big male bird emerge from a thicket about a hundred yards away. He stood still and stared at me for a few moments. I stared back. Then, expanding his short wings and with his tail erect, he came bounding towards me.

As I had nothing, not even a stick, with which to defend myself, I turned and ran towards the fence. But it was an unequal race. What were my steps of two or three feet against the creature's great strides of sixteen to twenty feet? There was only one hope: to get behind a large bush and try to elude the bird until help came. A dodging game was my only chance.

And so, I rushed for the nearest clump of thorn bushes and waited for my pursuer. The great bird wasted no time—he was immediately upon me.

Then the strangest encounter took place. I dodged this way and that, taking great care not to get directly in front of the ostrich's deadly kick. Ostriches kick forward, and with such terrific force that if you were struck, their huge chisel-like nails would cause you much damage.

I was breathless, and really quite helpless, calling wildly for help as I circled the thorn bush. My strength was ebbing. How much longer could I keep going? I was ready to drop from exhaustion.

As if aware of my condition, the infuriated bird suddenly doubled back on his course and charged straight at me. With a desperate effort I managed to step to one side. I don't know how, but I found myself holding on to one of the creature's wings, quite close to its body.

It was now the ostrich's turn to be frightened. He began to turn, or rather waltz, moving round and round so quickly that my feet were soon swinging out from his body, almost horizontally! All the while the ostrich kept opening and shutting his beak with loud snaps.

Imagine my situation as I clung desperately to the wing of the enraged bird. He was whirling me round and round as though he were a discus-thrower—and I the discus! My arms soon began to ache with the strain, and the swift and continuous circling was making me dizzy. But I knew that if I relaxed my hold, even for a second, a terrible fate awaited me.

Round and round we went in a great circle. It seemed as if that spiteful bird would never tire. And, I knew I could not hold on much longer. Suddenly, the ostrich went into reverse! This unexpected move made me lose my hold and sent me sprawling to the ground. I landed in a heap near the thorn bush and in an instant, before I even had time to realize what had happened, the big bird was upon me. I thought the end had come. Instinctively, I raised my hands to protect my face. But the ostrich did not strike.

I moved my hands from my face and there stood the creature with one foot raised, ready to deliver a deadly kick! I couldn't move. Was the bird going to play cat-and-mouse with me and prolong the agony?

As I watched, frightened and fascinated, the ostrich turned his head sharply to the left. A second later, he jumped back, turned, and made off as fast as he could go. Dazed, I wondered what had happened to make him beat so unexpected a retreat.

I soon found out. To my great joy, I heard the bark of my

truant dog, and the next moment he was jumping around me, licking my face and hands. Needless to say, I returned his caresses most affectionately! And I took good care to see that he did not leave my side until we were well clear of that ostrich 'camp'.

THE TIGER IN THE TUNNEL

Tembu, the boy, opened his eyes in the dark and wondered if his father was ready to leave the hut on his nightly errand. There was no moon that night, and the deathly stillness of the surrounding jungle was broken only occasionally by the shrill cry of a cicada. Sometimes from far off came the hollow hammering of a woodpecker, carried along on the faint breeze. Or the grunt of a wild boar could be heard as he dug up a favourite root. But these sounds were rare, and the silence of the forest always returned to swallow them up.

Baldeo, the watchman, was awake. He stretched himself, slowly unwinding the heavy shawl that covered him like a shroud. It was close on midnight and the chilly air made him shiver. The station, a small shack backed by heavy jungle, was a station only in name; for trains only stopped there, if at all, for a few seconds before entering the deep cutting that led to the tunnel. Most trains merely slowed down before taking the sharp curve before the cutting.

Baldeo was responsible for signalling whether or not the tunnel was clear of obstruction, and his hand-worked signal stood before the entrance. At night, it was his duty to see that the lamp was burning, and that the overland mail passed through safely.

'Shall I come too, Father?' asked Tembu sleepily, still lying huddled in a corner of the hut.

'No, it is cold tonight. Do not get up.'

Tembu, who was twelve, did not always sleep with his father at the station, for he also had to help in the home, where his mother and small sister were usually alone. They lived in a small tribal village on the outskirts of the forest, about three miles from the station. Their small rice fields did not provide them with more than a bare living, and Baldeo considered himself lucky to have got the job of *khalasi* at this small wayside signal-stop.

Still drowsy, Baldeo groped for his lamp in the darkness, then fumbled about in search of matches. When he had produced a light, he left the hut, closed the door behind him, and set off along the permanent way. Tembu had fallen asleep again.

Baldeo wondered whether the lamp on the signal post was still alight. Gathering his shawl closer about him, he stumbled on, sometimes along the rails, sometimes along the ballast. He longed to get back to his warm corner in the hut.

The eeriness of the place was increased by the neighbouring hills, which overhung the main line threateningly. On entering the cutting, with its sheer rock walls towering high above the rails, Baldeo could not help thinking about the wild animals he might encounter. He had heard many tales of the famous tunnel tiger, a man-eater who was supposed to frequent this spot; but he hardly believed these stories for, since his arrival at this place a month ago, he had not seen or even heard a tiger.

There had, of course, been panthers, and only a few days previously the villagers had killed one with their spears and axes. Baldeo had occasionally heard the sawing of a panther calling to its mate, but they had not come near the tunnel or shed.

Baldeo walked confidently for, being a tribal himself, he was used to the jungle and its ways. Like his forefathers, he carried a small axe, fragile to look at, but deadly when in use. With it, in three or four swift strokes, he could cut down a tree as neatly as if it had been sawn; and he prided himself on his skill in wielding it against wild animals. He had killed a young boar with it once, and the family had feasted on the flesh for three days. The axe-head of pure steel, thin but ringing true like a bell, had been made by his father over a charcoal fire. This axe was a part of himself, and wherever he went, be it to the local market seven miles away, or to a tribal dance, the axe was always in his hand. Occasionally, an official who had come to the station had offered him good money for the weapon; but Baldeo had no intention of parting with it.

The cutting curved sharply, and in the darkness, the black entrance to the tunnel loomed up menacingly. The signal light was out. Baldeo set to work to haul the lamp down by its chain. If the oil had finished, he would have to return to the hut for more. The mail train was due in five minutes.

Once more he fumbled for his matches. Then suddenly he stood still and listened. The frightened cry of a barking deer, followed by a crashing sound in the undergrowth, made Baldeo hurry. There was still a little oil in the lamp, and after an instant's hesitation he lit the lamp again and hoisted it back into position. Having done this, he walked quickly down the tunnel, swinging his own lamp, so that the shadows leapt up and down the soot-stained walls, and having made sure that the line was clear, he returned to the entrance and sat down to wait for the mail train.

The train was late. Sitting huddled up, almost dozing, he soon forgot his surroundings and began to nod off.

Back in the hut, the trembling of the ground told of the approach of the train, and a low, distant rumble woke the boy, who sat up, rubbing the sleep from his eyes.

'Father, it's time to light the lamp,' he mumbled, and then, realizing that his father had been gone some time, he lay down again; but he was wide awake now, waiting for the train to pass, waiting for his father's returning footsteps.

A low grunt resounded from the top of the cutting. In a second Baldeo was awake, all his senses alert. Only a tiger could emit such a sound.

There was no shelter for Baldeo, but he grasped his axe firmly and tensed his body, trying to make out the direction from which the animal was approaching. For some time there was only silence, even the usual jungle noises seemed to have ceased altogether. Then a thump and the rattle of small stones announced that the tiger had sprung into the cutting.

Baldeo, listening as he had never listened before, wondered if it was making for the tunnel or the opposite direction—the direction of the hut, in which Tembu would be lying unprotected. He did not have to wonder for long. Before a minute had passed, he made out the huge body of the tiger trotting steadily towards him. Its eyes shone a brilliant green in the light from the signal lamp. Flight was useless, for in the dark, the tiger would be more sure-footed than Baldeo and would soon be upon him from behind. Baldeo stood with his back to the signal post, motionless, staring at the great brute moving rapidly towards him. The tiger, used to the ways of men, for it had been preying on them for years, came on fearlessly, and with a quick run and a snarl struck out with its right paw, expecting to bowl over this puny man who dared stand in the way.

Baldeo, however, was ready. With a marvellously agile leap he avoided the paw and brought his axe down on the animal's shoulder. The tiger gave a roar and attempted to close in. Again Baldeo drove his axe with true aim; but, to his horror, the beast swerved, and the axe caught the tiger on the shoulder, almost severing the leg. To make matters worse, the axe remained stuck in the bone, and Baldeo was left without a weapon.

The tiger, roaring with pain, now sprang upon Baldeo, bringing him down and then tearing at his broken body. It was all over in a few minutes. Baldeo was conscious only of a searing pain down his back, and then there was blackness and the night closed in on him forever.

The tiger drew off and sat down licking his wounded leg, roaring every now and then with agony. He did not notice the faint rumble that shook the earth, followed by the distant puffing of an engine steadily climbing. The overland mail was approaching. Through the trees beyond the cutting, as the train advanced, the glow of the furnace could be seen; and showers of sparks fell like Diwali lights over the forest.

As the train entered the cutting, the engine whistled once, loud and piercingly. The tiger raised his head, then slowly got to his feet. He found himself trapped like the man. Flight along the cutting was impossible. He entered the tunnel, running as fast as his wounded leg would carry him. And then, with a roar and a shower of sparks, the train entered the yawning tunnel. The noise in the confined space was deafening; but, when the train came out into the open, on the other side, silence returned once more to the forest and the tunnel.

At the next station, the driver slowed down and stopped his train to water the engine. He got down to stretch his legs and decided to examine the head-lamps. He received the surprise of his life; for, just above the cowcatcher lay the major portion of the tiger, cut in half by the engine.

There was considerable excitement and conjecture at the station, but back at the cutting there was no sound except for the sobs of the boy as he sat beside the body of his father. He sat there a long time, unafraid of the darkness, guarding the body from jackals and hyenas, until the first faint light of dawn brought with it the arrival of the relief watchman.

Tembu and his sister and mother were plunged in grief for two whole days; but life had to go on, and a living had to be made, and all the responsibility now fell on Tembu. Three nights later, he was at the cutting, lighting the signal lamp for the overland mail.

He sat down in the darkness to wait for the train, and sang softly to himself. There was nothing to be afraid of—his father had killed the tiger, the forest gods were pleased; and besides, he had the axe with him, his father's axe, and he knew how to use it.

PANTHER'S MOON

I

In the entire village, he was the first to get up. Even the dog, a big hill mastiff called Sheroo, was asleep in a corner of the dark room, curled up near the cold embers of the previous night's fire. Bisnu's tousled head emerged from his blanket. He rubbed the sleep from his eyes and sat up on his haunches. Then, gathering his wits, he crawled in the direction of the loud ticking that came from the battered little clock which occupied the second most honoured place in a niche in the wall. The most honoured place belonged to a picture of Ganesha, the god of learning, who had an elephant's head and a fat boy's body.

Bringing his face close to the clock, Bisnu could just make out the hands. It was five o'clock. He had half an hour in which to get ready and leave.

He got up, in vest and underpants, and moved quietly towards the door. The soft tread of his bare feet woke Sheroo, and the big black dog rose silently and padded behind the boy. The door opened and closed, and then the boy and the dog were outside in the early dawn. The month was June, and the nights were warm, even in the Himalayan valleys; but there was fresh dew on the grass. Bisnu felt the dew beneath his feet. He took a deep breath and began walking down to the stream.

The sound of the stream filled the small valley. At that early hour of the morning, it was the only sound; but Bisnu was hardly conscious of it. It was a sound he lived with and took for granted. It was only when he had crossed the hill, on his way to the town—and the sound of the stream grew distant—that he really began to notice it. And it was only when the stream was too far away to be heard that he really missed its sound.

He slipped out of his underclothes, gazed for a few moments at the goose pimples rising on his flesh, and then dashed into the shallow stream. As he went further in, the cold mountain water reached his loins and navel, and he gasped with shock and pleasure. He drifted slowly with the current, swam across to a small inlet which formed a fairly deep pool and plunged into the water. Sheroo hated cold water at this early hour. Had the sun been up, he would not have hesitated to join Bisnu. Now he contented himself with sitting on a smooth rock and gazing placidly at the slim brown boy splashing about in the clear water, in the widening light of dawn.

Bisnu did not stay long in the water. There wasn't time. When he returned to the house, he found his mother up, making tea and chapattis. His sister, Puja, was still asleep. She was a little older than Bisnu, a pretty girl with large black eyes, good teeth and strong arms and legs. During the day, she helped her mother in the house and in the fields. She did not go to the school with Bisnu. But when he came home in the evenings, he would try teaching her some of the things he had learnt. Their father was dead. Bisnu, at twelve, considered himself the head of the family.

He ate two chapattis, after spreading butter-oil on them. He drank a glass of hot sweet tea. His mother gave two thick chapattis to Sheroo, and the dog wolfed them down in a few minutes. Then she wrapped two chapattis and a gourd curry in some big green leaves, and handed these to Bisnu. This was his lunch packet. His mother and Puja would take their meal afterwards.

When Bisnu was dressed, he stood with folded hands before the picture of Ganesha. Ganesha is the god who blesses all beginnings. The author who begins to write a new book, the banker who opens a new ledger, the traveller who starts on a journey, all invoke the kindly help of Ganesha. And as Bisnu made a journey every day, he never left without the goodwill of the elephant-headed god.

How, one might ask, did Ganesha get his elephant's head?

When born, he was a beautiful child. Parvati, his mother, was so proud of him that she went about showing him to everyone. Unfortunately, she made the mistake of showing the child to that envious planet, Saturn, who promptly burnt off poor Ganesha's head. Parvati in despair went to Brahma, the Creator, for a new head for her son. He had no head to give her, but advised her to search for some man or animal caught in a sinful or wrong act. Parvati wandered about until she came upon an elephant sleeping with its head the wrong way, that is, to the south. She promptly removed the elephant's head and planted it on Ganesha's shoulders, where it took root.

Bisnu knew this story. He had heard it from his mother.

Wearing a white shirt and black shorts, and a pair of worn white keds, he was ready for his long walk to school, five miles up the mountain.

His sister woke up just as he was about to leave. She pushed the hair away from her face and gave Bisnu one of her rare smiles.

'I hope you have not forgotten,' she said.

'Forgotten?' said Bisnu, pretending innocence. 'Is there anything I am supposed to remember?'

'Don't tease me. You promised to buy me a pair of bangles, remember? I hope you won't spend the money on sweets, as you did last time.'

'Oh, yes, your bangles,' said Bisnu. 'Girls have nothing better to do than waste money on trinkets. Now, don't lose your temper! I'll get them for you. Red and gold are the colours you want?'

'Yes, Brother,' said Puja gently, pleased that Bisnu had remembered the colours. 'And for your dinner tonight we'll make you something special. Won't we, Mother?'

'Yes. But hurry up and dress. There is some ploughing to be done today. The rains will soon be here, if the gods are kind.'

'The monsoon will be late this year,' said Bisnu. 'Mr Nautiyal, our teacher, told us so. He said it had nothing to do with the gods.'

'Be off, you are getting late,' said Puja, before Bisnu could begin an argument with his mother. She was diligently winding the old clock. It was quite light in the room. The sun would be up any minute.

Bisnu shouldered his school bag, kissed his mother, pinched his sister's cheeks and left the house. He started climbing the steep path up the mountainside. Sheroo bounded ahead; for he, too, always went with Bisnu to school.

Five miles to school. Every day, except Sunday, Bisnu walked five miles to school; and in the evening, he walked home again. There was no school in his own small village of Manjari, for the village consisted of only five families. The nearest school was at Kemptee, a small township on the bus route through the district of Garhwal. A number of boys walked to school, from distances of two or three miles; their villages were not quite as remote as Manjari. But Bisnu's village lay right at the bottom of the mountain, a drop of over two thousand feet from Kemptee. There was no proper road between the village and the town.

In Kemptee there was a school, a small mission hospital, a post office and several shops. In Manjari village there were none of these amenities. If you were sick, you stayed at home until you got well; if you were very sick, you walked or were carried to the hospital, up the five mile path. If you wanted to buy something, you went without it; but if you wanted it very badly, you could walk the five miles to Kemptee.

Manjari was known as the Five Mile Village.

Twice a week, if there were any letters, a postman came to the village. Bisnu usually passed the postman on his way to and from school.

There were other boys in Manjari village, but Bisnu was the only one who went to school. His mother would not have fussed if he had stayed at home and worked in the fields. That was what the other boys did; all except lazy Chittru, who preferred fishing in the stream or helping himself to the fruit of other people's trees. But Bisnu went to school. He went because he wanted to. No one could force him to go; and no one could stop him from going. He had set his heart on receiving a good schooling. He wanted to read and write as well as anyone in the big world, the world that seemed to begin only where the mountains ended. He felt cut off from the world in his small valley. He would rather live at the top of a mountain than at the bottom of one. That was why he liked climbing to Kemptee, it took him to the top of the mountain; and from its ridge he could look down on his own valley to the north, and on the wide endless plains stretching towards the south.

The plainsman looks to the hills for the needs of his spirit but the hill man looks to the plains for a living.

Leaving the village and the fields below him, Bisnu climbed steadily up the bare hillside, now dry and brown. By the time the sun was up, he had entered the welcome shade of an oak and rhododendron forest. Sheroo went bounding ahead, chasing squirrels and barking at langurs.

A colony of langurs lived in the oak forest. They fed on oak leaves, acorns and other green things, and usually remained in the trees, coming down to the ground only to play or bask in the sun. They were beautiful, supple-limbed animals, with black faces and silver-grey coats and long, sensitive tails. They leapt from tree to tree with great agility. The young ones wrestled on the grass like boys.

A dignified community, the langurs did not have the cheekiness or dishonest habits of the red monkeys of the plains; they did not approach dogs or humans. But they had grown used to Bisnu's comings and goings, and did not fear him. Some of the older ones would watch him quietly, a little puzzled. They did not go near the town, because the Kemptee boys threw stones at them. And anyway, the oak forest gave them all the food they required.

Emerging from the trees, Bisnu crossed a small brook. Here he stopped to drink the fresh clean water of a spring. The brook tumbled down the mountain and joined the river a little below Bisnu's village. Coming from another direction was a second path, and at the junction of the two paths Sarru was waiting for him.

Sarru came from a small village about three miles from Bisnu's and closer to the town. He had two large milk cans slung over his shoulders. Every morning he carried this milk to town, selling one can to the school and the other to Mrs Taylor, the lady doctor at the small mission hospital. He was a little older than Bisnu but not as well-built.

They hailed each other, and Sarru fell into step beside Bisnu. They often met at this spot, keeping each other company for the remaining two miles to Kemptee.

'There was a panther in our village last night,' said Sarru.

This information interested but did not excite Bisnu. Panthers were common enough in the hills and did not usually present a problem except during the winter months, when their natural prey was scarce. Then, occasionally, a panther would take to haunting the outskirts of a village, seizing a careless dog or a stray goat.

'Did you lose any animals?' asked Bisnu.

'No. It tried to get into the cowshed but the dogs set up an alarm. We drove it off.'

'It must be the same one which came around last winter. We lost a calf and two dogs in our village.'

'Wasn't that the one the shikaris wounded? I hope it hasn't become a cattle lifter.'

'It could be the same. It has a bullet in its leg. These hunters are the people who cause all the trouble. They think it's easy to shoot a panther. It would be better if they missed altogether, but they usually wound it.'

'And then the panther's too slow to catch the barking deer, and starts on our own animals.'

'We're lucky it didn't become a man-eater. Do you remember the man-eater six years ago? I was very small then. My father told me all about it. Ten people were killed in our valley alone. What happened to it?'

'I don't know. Some say it poisoned itself when it ate the headman of another village.'

Bisnu laughed. 'No one liked that old villain. He must have been a man-eater himself in some previous existence!' They linked arms and scrambled up the stony path. Sheroo began barking and ran ahead. Someone was coming down the path.

It was Mela Ram, the postman.

II

'Any letters for us?' asked Bisnu and Sarru together.

They never received any letters but that did not stop them from asking. It was one way of finding out who had received letters.

'You're welcome to all of them,' said Mela Ram, 'if you'll carry my bag for me.'

'Not today,' said Sarru. 'We're busy today. Is there a letter from Corporal Ghanshyam for his family?'

'Yes, there is a postcard for his people. He is posted on the Ladakh border now and finds it very cold there.'

Postcards, unlike sealed letters, were considered public property and were read by everyone. The senders knew that too, and so Corporal Ghanshyam Singh was careful to mention that he expected a promotion very soon. He wanted everyone in his village to know it.

Mela Ram, complaining of sore feet, continued on his way, and the boys carried on up the path. It was eight o'clock when they reached Kemptee. Dr Taylor's outpatients were just beginning to trickle in at the hospital gate. The doctor was trying to prop up a rose creeper which had blown down during the night. She liked attending to her plants in the mornings, before starting on her patients. She found this helped her in her work. There was a lot in common between ailing plants and ailing people.

Dr Taylor was fifty, white-haired but fresh in the face and full of vitality. She had been in India for twenty years, and ten of these had been spent working in the hill regions.

She saw Bisnu coming down the road. She knew about the boy and his long walk to school and admired him for his keenness and sense of purpose. She wished there were more like him.

Bisnu greeted her shyly. Sheroo barked and put his paws up on the gate.

'Yes, there's a bone for you,' said Dr Taylor. She often put aside bones for the big black dog, for she knew that Bisnu's people could not afford to give the dog a regular diet of meat—though he did well enough on milk and chapattis.

She threw the bone over the gate and Sheroo caught it

before it fell. The school bell began ringing and Bisnu broke into a run. Sheroo loped along behind the boy.

When Bisnu entered the school gate, Sheroo sat down on the grass of the compound. He would remain there until the lunch break. He knew of various ways of amusing himself during school hours and had friends among the bazaar dogs. But just then he didn't want company. He had his bone to get on with.

Mr Nautiyal, Bisnu's teacher, was in a bad mood. He was a keen rose grower and only that morning, on getting up and looking out of his bedroom window, he had been horrified to see a herd of goats in his garden. He had chased them down the road with a stick but the damage had already been done. His prize roses had all been consumed.

Mr Nautiyal had been so upset that he had gone without his breakfast. He had also cut himself whilst shaving. Thus, his mood had gone from bad to worse. Several times during the day, he brought down his ruler on the knuckles of any boy who irritated him. Bisnu was one of his best pupils. But even Bisnu irritated him by asking too many questions about a new sum which Mr Nautiyal didn't feel like explaining.

That was the kind of day it was for Mr Nautiyal. Most school teachers know similar days.

Poor Mr Nautiyal, thought Bisnu. *I wonder why he's so upset. It must be because of his pay. He doesn't get much money. But he's a good teacher. I hope he doesn't take another job.*

But after Mr Nautiyal had eaten his lunch, his mood improved (as it always did after a meal), and the rest of the day passed serenely. Armed with a bundle of homework, Bisnu came out from the school compound at four o'clock, and was immediately joined by Sheroo. He proceeded down the road in the company of several of his classfellows. But he did not linger long in the bazaar. There were five miles to walk, and he did not like to get home too late. Usually, he reached his house just as it was beginning to get dark.

Sarru had gone home long ago, and Bisnu had to make the return journey on his own. It was a good opportunity to memorize the words of an English poem he had been asked to learn.

Bisnu had reached the little brook when he remembered the bangles he had promised to buy for his sister.

'Oh, I've forgotten them again,' he said aloud. 'Now I'll catch it—and she's probably made something special for my dinner!'

Sheroo, to whom these words were addressed, paid no attention but bounded off into the oak forest. Bisnu looked around for the monkeys but they were nowhere to be seen.

Strange, he thought, *I wonder why they have disappeared.*

He was startled by a sudden sharp cry, followed by a fierce yelp. He knew at once that Sheroo was in trouble. The noise came from the bushes down the khud, into which the dog had rushed but a few seconds previously.

Bisnu jumped off the path and ran down the slope towards the bushes. There was no dog and not a sound. He whistled and called, but there was no response. Then he saw something lying on the dry grass. He picked it up. It was a portion of a dog's collar, stained with blood. It was Sheroo's collar and Sheroo's blood.

Bisnu did not search further. He knew, without a doubt, that Sheroo had been seized by a panther. No other animal could have attacked so silently and swiftly and carried off a big dog without a struggle. Sheroo was dead—must have been dead within seconds of being caught and flung into the air. Bisnu knew the danger that lay in wait for him if he followed the blood trail through the trees. The panther would attack anyone who interfered with its meal.

With tears starting in his eyes, Bisnu carried on down the path to the village. His fingers still clutched the little bit of bloodstained collar that was all that was left to him of his dog.

III

Bisnu was not a very sentimental boy, but he sorrowed for his dog who had been his companion on many a hike into the hills and forests. He did not sleep that night, but turned restlessly from side to side moaning softly. After some time he felt Puja's hand on his head. She began stroking his brow. He took her hand in his own and the clasp of her rough, warm familiar hand gave him a feeling of comfort and security.

Next morning, when he went down to the stream to bathe, he missed the presence of his dog. He did not stay long in the water. It wasn't as much fun when there was no Sheroo to watch him.

When Bisnu's mother gave him his food, she told him to be careful and hurry home that evening. A panther, even if it is only a cowardly lifter of sheep or dogs, is not to be trifled with. And this particular panther had shown some daring by seizing the dog even before it was dark.

Still, there was no question of staying away from school. If Bisnu remained at home every time a panther put in an appearance, he might as well stop going to school altogether.

He set off even earlier than usual and reached the meeting of the paths long before Sarru. He did not wait for his friend, because he did not feel like talking about the loss of his dog. It was not the day for the postman, and so Bisnu reached Kemptee without meeting anyone on the way. He tried creeping past the hospital gate unnoticed, but Dr Taylor saw him and the first thing she said was: 'Where's Sheroo? I've got something for him.'

When Dr Taylor saw the boy's face, she knew at once that something was wrong.

'What is it, Bisnu?' she asked. She looked quickly up and down the road. 'Is it Sheroo?'

He nodded gravely.

'A panther took him,' he said.

'In the village?'

'No, while we were walking home through the forest. I did not see anything—but I heard.'

Dr Taylor knew that there was nothing she could say that would console him, and she tried to conceal the bone which she had brought out for the dog, but Bisnu noticed her hiding it behind her back and the tears welled up in his eyes. He turned away and began running down the road.

His schoolfellows noticed Sheroo's absence and questioned Bisnu. He had to tell them everything. They were full of sympathy, but they were also quite thrilled at what had happened and kept pestering Bisnu for all the details. There was a lot of noise in the classroom, and Mr Nautiyal had to call for order. When he learnt what had happened, he patted Bisnu on the head and told him that he need not attend school for the rest of the day. But Bisnu did not want to go home. After school, he got into a fight with one of the boys, and that helped him forget.

IV

The panther that plunged the village into an atmosphere of gloom and terror may not have been the same panther that took Sheroo. There was no way of knowing, and it would have made no difference, because the panther that came by night and struck at the people of Manjari was that most feared of wild creatures, a man-eater.

Nine-year-old Sanjay, son of Kalam Singh, was the first child to be attacked by the panther.

Kalam Singh's house was the last in the village and nearest the stream. Like the other houses, it was quite small, just a room above and a stable below, with steps leading up from outside the house. He lived there with his wife, two sons (Sanjay was the youngest) and little daughter Basanti who had just turned three.

Sanjay had brought his father's cows home after grazing them on the hillside in the company of other children. He had also brought home an edible wild plant, which his mother cooked into a tasty dish for their evening meal. They had their food at dusk, sitting on the floor of their single room, and soon after, settled down for the night. Sanjay curled up in his favourite spot, with his head near the door, where he got a little fresh air. As the nights were warm, the door was usually left a little ajar. Sanjay's mother piled ash on the embers of the fire and the family was soon asleep.

No one heard the stealthy padding of a panther approaching the door, pushing it wide open. But suddenly there were sounds of a frantic struggle, and Sanjay's stifled cries were mixed with the grunts of the panther. Kalam Singh leapt to his feet with a shout. The panther had dragged Sanjay out of the door and was pulling him down the steps, when Kalam Singh started battering at the animal with a large stone. The rest of the family screamed in terror, rousing the entire village. A number of men came to Kalam Singh's assistance, and the panther was driven off. But Sanjay lay unconscious.

Someone brought a lantern and the boy's mother screamed when she saw her small son with his head lying in a pool of blood. It looked as if the side of his head had been eaten off by the panther. But he was still alive, and as Kalam Singh plastered ash on the boy's head to stop the bleeding, he found that though the scalp had been torn off one side of the head, the bare bone was smooth and unbroken.

'He won't live through the night,' said a neighbour. 'We'll have to carry him down to the river in the morning.'

The dead were always cremated on the banks of a small river which flowed past Manjari village.

Suddenly the panther, still prowling about the village, called out in rage and frustration, and the villagers rushed to their homes in panic and barricaded themselves in for the night.

Sanjay's mother sat by the boy for the rest of the night, weeping and watching. Towards dawn he started to moan and show signs of coming round. At this sign of returning consciousness, Kalam Singh rose determinedly and looked around for his stick.

He told his elder son to remain behind with the mother and daughter, as he was going to take Sanjay to Dr Taylor at the hospital.

'See, he is moaning and in pain,' said Kalam Singh. 'That means he has a chance to live if he can be treated at once.'

With a stout stick in his hand, and Sanjay on his back, Kalam Singh set off on the two miles of hard mountain track to the hospital at Kemptee. His son, a bloodstained cloth around his head, was moaning but still unconscious. When at last Kalam Singh climbed up through the last fields below the hospital, he asked for the doctor and stammered out an account of what had happened.

It was a terrible injury, as Dr Taylor discovered. The bone over almost one-third of the head was bare and the scalp was torn all round. As the father told his story, the doctor cleaned and dressed the wound, and then gave Sanjay a shot of penicillin to prevent sepsis. Later, Kalam Singh carried the boy home again.

V

After this, the panther went away for some time. But the people of Manjari could not be sure of its whereabouts. They kept to their houses after dark and shut their doors. Bisnu had to stop going to school, because there was no one to accompany him and it was dangerous to go alone. This worried him, because his final exam was only a few weeks off and he would be missing important classwork. When he wasn't in the fields, helping with the sowing of rice and maize, he would be sitting in the shade of a chestnut tree, going through his well-thumbed second-hand school books. He had no other reading, except for a copy of the Ramayana and a Hindi translation of *Alice's Adventures in Wonderland.* These were well-preserved, read only in fits and starts, and usually kept locked in his mother's old tin trunk.

Sanjay had nightmares for several nights and woke up screaming. But with the resilience of youth, he quickly recovered. At the end of the week he was able to walk to the hospital, though his father always accompanied him. Even a desperate panther will hesitate to attack a party of two. Sanjay, with his thin little face and huge bandaged head, looked a pathetic figure, but he was getting better and the wound looked healthy.

Bisnu often went to see him, and the two boys spent long hours together near the stream. Sometimes Chittru would join them, and they would try catching fish with a home-made net. They were often successful in taking home one or two mountain trout. Sometimes, Bisnu and Chittru wrestled in the shallow water or on the grassy banks of the stream. Chittru was a chubby boy with a broad chest, strong legs and thighs, and when he used his weight he got Bisnu under him. But Bisnu was hard and wiry and had very strong wrists and fingers. When he had

Chittru in a vice, the bigger boy would cry out and give up the struggle. Sanjay could not join in these games.

He had never been a very strong boy and he needed plenty of rest if his wounds were to heal well.

The panther had not been seen for over a week, and the people of Manjari were beginning to hope that it might have moved on over the mountain or further down the valley.

'I think I can start going to school again,' said Bisnu. 'The panther has gone away.'

'Don't be too sure,' said Puja. 'The moon is full these days and perhaps it is only being cautious.'

'Wait a few days,' said their mother. 'It is better to wait. Perhaps you could go the day after tomorrow when Sanjay goes to the hospital with his father. Then you will not be alone.'

And so, two days later, Bisnu went up to Kemptee with Sanjay and Kalam Singh. Sanjay's wound had almost healed over. Little islets of flesh had grown over the bone. Dr Taylor told him that he need come to see her only once a fortnight, instead of every third day.

Bisnu went to his school, and was given a warm welcome by his friends and by Mr Nautiyal.

'You'll have to work hard,' said his teacher. 'You have to catch up with the others. If you like, I can give you some extra time after classes.'

'Thank you, sir, but it will make me late,' said Bisnu. 'I must get home before it is dark, otherwise my mother will worry. I think the panther has gone but nothing is certain.'

'Well, you mustn't take risks. Do your best, Bisnu. Work hard and you'll soon catch up with your lessons.'

Sanjay and Kalam Singh were waiting for him outside the school. Together they took the path down to Manjari, passing the postman on the way. Mela Ram said he had heard that the panther was in another district and that there was nothing to fear. He was on his rounds again.

Nothing happened on the way. The langurs were back in their favourite part of the forest. Bisnu got home just as the kerosene lamp was being lit. Puja met him at the door with a winsome smile.

'Did you get the bangles?' she asked.

But Bisnu had forgotten again.

VI

There had been a thunderstorm and some rain—a short, sharp shower which gave the villagers hope that the monsoon would arrive on time. It brought out the thunder lilies—pink, crocus-like flowers which sprang up on the hillsides immediately after a summer shower.

Bisnu, on his way home from school, was caught in the rain. He knew the shower would not last, so he took shelter in a small cave and, to pass the time, began doing sums, scratching figures in the damp earth with the end of a stick.

When the rain stopped, he came out from the cave and continued down the path. He wasn't in a hurry. The rain had made everything smell fresh and good. The scent from fallen pine needles rose from wet earth. The leaves of the oak trees had been washed clean and a light breeze turned them about, showing their silver undersides. The birds, refreshed and high-spirited, set up a terrific noise. The worst offenders were the yellow-bottomed bulbuls who squabbled and fought in the blackberry bushes. A barbet, high up in the branches of a deodar, set up its querulous, plaintive call. And a flock of bright green parrots came swooping down the hill to settle in a wild plum tree and feast on the unripe fruit. The langurs, too, had been revived by the rain. They leapt friskily from tree to tree greeting Bisnu with little grunts.

He was almost out of the oak forest when he heard a faint bleating. Presently, a little goat came stumbling up the path towards him. The kid was far from home and must have strayed from the rest of the herd. But it was not yet conscious of being lost. It came to Bisnu with a hop, skip and a jump and started nuzzling against his legs like a cat.

'I wonder who you belong to,' mused Bisnu, stroking the little creature. 'You'd better come home with me until someone claims you.'

He didn't have to take the kid in his arms. It was used to humans and followed close at his heels. Now that darkness was coming on, Bisnu walked a little faster.

He had not gone very far when he heard the sawing grunt of a panther.

The sound came from the hill to the right, and Bisnu judged the distance to be anything from 100 to 200 yards. He hesitated on the path, wondering what to do. Then he picked the kid up in his arms and hurried on in the direction of home and safety.

The panther called again, much closer now. If it was an ordinary panther, it would go away on finding that the kid was with Bisnu. If it was the man-eater, it would not hesitate to attack the boy, for no man-eater fears a human. There was no time to lose and there did not seem much point in running. Bisnu looked up and down the hillside. The forest was far behind him and there were only a few trees in his vicinity. He chose a spruce.

The branches of the Himalayan spruce are very brittle and snap easily beneath a heavy weight. They were strong enough to support Bisnu's light frame. It was unlikely they would take the weight of a full-grown panther. At least that was what Bisnu hoped.

Holding the kid with one arm, Bisnu gripped a low branch and swung himself up into the tree. He was a good climber.

Slowly but confidently he climbed halfway up the tree, until he was about twelve feet above the ground. He couldn't go any higher without risking a fall.

He had barely settled himself in the crook of a branch when the panther came into the open, running into the clearing at a brisk trot. This was no stealthy approach, no wary stalking of its prey. It was the man-eater, all right. Bisnu felt a cold shiver run down his spine. He felt a little sick.

The panther stood in the clearing with a slight thrusting forward of the head. This gave it the appearance of gazing intently and rather short-sightedly at some invisible object in the clearing. But there is nothing short-sighted about a panther's vision. Its sight and hearing are acute.

Bisnu remained motionless in the tree and sent up a prayer to all the gods he could think of. But the kid began bleating. The panther looked up and gave its deep-throated, rasping grunt—a fearsome sound, calculated to strike terror in any treeborne animal. Many a monkey, petrified by a panther's roar, has fallen from its perch to make a meal for Mr Spots. The man-eater was trying the same technique on Bisnu. But though the boy was trembling with fright, he clung firmly to the base of the spruce tree.

The panther did not make any attempt to leap into the tree. Perhaps, it knew instinctively that this was not the type of tree that it could climb. Instead, it described a semicircle round the tree, keeping its face turned towards Bisnu. Then it disappeared into the bushes.

The man-eater was cunning. It hoped to put the boy off his guard, perhaps entice him down from the tree. For, a few seconds later, with a half-humorous growl, it rushed back into the clearing and then stopped, staring up at the boy in some surprise. The panther was getting frustrated. It snarled, and putting its forefeet up against the tree trunk began scratching at the bark in the manner of an ordinary domestic cat. The tree shook at each thud of the beast's paw.

Bisnu began shouting for help.

The moon had not yet come up. Down in Manjari village, Bisnu's mother and sister stood in their lighted doorway, gazing anxiously up the pathway. Every now and then, Puja would turn to take a look at the small clock.

Sanjay's father appeared in a field below. He had a kerosene lantern in his hand.

'Sister, isn't your boy home as yet?' he asked.

'No, he hasn't arrived. We are very worried. He should have been home an hour ago. Do you think the panther will be about tonight? There's going to be a moon.'

'True, but it will be dark for another hour. I will fetch the other menfolk, and we will go up the mountain for your boy. There may have been a landslide during the rain. Perhaps the path has been washed away.'

'Thank you, brother. But arm yourselves, just in case the panther is about.'

'I will take my spear,' said Kalam Singh. 'I have sworn to spear that devil when I find him. There is some evil spirit dwelling in the beast and it must be destroyed!'

'I am coming with you,' said Puja.

'No, you cannot go,' said her mother. 'It's bad enough that Bisnu is in danger. You stay at home with me. This is work for men.'

'I shall be safe with them,' insisted Puja. 'I am going, Mother!' And she jumped down the embankment into the field and followed Sanjay's father through the village.

Ten minutes later, two men armed with axes had joined Kalam Singh in the courtyard of his house, and the small party moved silently and swiftly up the mountain path. Puja walked in the middle of the group, holding the lantern. As soon as the village lights were hidden by a shoulder of the hill, the men began to shout—both to frighten the panther, if it was about, and to give themselves courage.

Bisnu's mother closed the front door and turned to the image of Ganesha, the god for comfort and help.

Bisnu's calls were carried on the wind, and Puja and the men heard him while they were still half a mile away. Their own shouts increased in volume and, hearing their voices, Bisnu felt strength return to his shaking limbs. Emboldened by the approach of his own people, he began shouting insults at the snarling panther, then throwing twigs and small branches at the enraged animal. The kid added its bleats to the boy's shouts, the birds took up the chorus. The langurs squealed and grunted, the searchers shouted themselves hoarse, and the panther howled with rage. The forest had never before been so noisy.

As the search party drew near, they could hear the panther's savage snarls, and hurried, fearing that perhaps Bisnu had been seized. Puja began to run.

'Don't rush ahead, girl,' said Kalam Singh. 'Stay between us.'

The panther, now aware of the approaching humans, stood still in the middle of the clearing, head thrust forward in a familiar stance. There seemed too many men for one panther. When the animal saw the light of the lantern dancing between the trees, it turned, snarled defiance and hate, and without another look at the boy in the tree, disappeared into the bushes. It was not yet ready for a showdown.

VII

Nobody turned up to claim the little goat, so Bisnu kept it. A goat was a poor substitute for a dog, but, like Mary's lamb, it followed Bisnu wherever he went, and the boy couldn't help being touched by its devotion. He took it down to the stream, where it would skip about in the shallows and nibble the sweet grass that grew on the banks.

As for the panther, frustrated in its attempt on Bisnu's life, it did not wait long before attacking another human.

It was Chittru who came running down the path one afternoon, bubbling excitedly about the panther and the postman.

Chittru, deeming it safe to gather ripe bilberries in the daytime, had walked about half a mile up the path from the village, when he had stumbled across Mela Ram's mailbag lying on the ground. Of the postman himself there was no sign. But a trail of blood led through the bushes.

Once again, a party of men headed by Kalam Singh and accompanied by Bisnu and Chittru, went out to look for the postman. But though they found Mela Ram's bloodstained clothes, they could not find his body. The panther had made no mistake this time.

It was to be several weeks before Manjari had a new postman.

A few days after Mela Ram's disappearance, an old woman was sleeping with her head near the open door of her house. She had been advised to sleep inside with the door closed, but the nights were hot and anyway the old woman was a little deaf, and in the middle of the night, an hour before moonrise, the panther seized her by the throat. Her strangled cry woke her grown-up son, and all the men in the village woke up at his shouts and came running.

The panther dragged the old woman out of the house and down the steps, but left her when the men approached with their axes and spears, and made off into the bushes. The old woman was still alive, and the men made a rough stretcher of bamboo and vines and started carrying her up the path. But they had not gone far when she began to cough, and because of her terrible throat wounds, her lungs collapsed and she died.

It was the 'dark of the month'—the week of the new moon when nights are darkest.

Bisnu, closing the front door and lighting the kerosene lantern, said, 'I wonder where that panther is tonight!'

The panther was busy in another village: Sarru's village.

A woman and her daughter had been out in the evening bedding the cattle down in the stable. The girl had gone into the house and the woman was following. As she bent down to go in at the low door, the panther sprang from the bushes. Fortunately, one of its paws hit the doorpost and broke the force of the attack, or the woman would have been killed. When she cried out, the men came round shouting and the panther slunk off. The woman had deep scratches on her back and was badly shocked.

The next day, a small party of villagers presented themselves in front of the magistrate's office at Kemptee and demanded that something be done about the panther. But the magistrate was away on tour, and there was no one else in Kemptee who had a gun. Mr Nautiyal met the villagers and promised to write to a well-known shikari, but said that it would be at least a fortnight before the shikari would be able to come.

Bisnu was fretting because he could not go to school. Most boys would be only too happy to miss school, but when you are living in a remote village in the mountains and having an education is the only way of seeing the world, you look forward to going to school, even if it is five miles from home. Bisnu's exams were only two weeks off, and he didn't want to remain in the same class while the others were promoted. Besides, he knew he could pass even though he had missed a number of lessons. But he had to sit for the exams. He couldn't miss them.

'Cheer up, Bhaiya,' said Puja, as they sat drinking glasses

of hot tea after their evening meal. 'The panther may go away once the rains break.'

'Even the rains are late this year,' said Bisnu. 'It's so hot and dry. Can't we open the door?'

'And be dragged down the steps by the panther?' said his mother. 'It isn't safe to have the window open, let alone the door.' And she went to the small window—through which a cat would have found difficulty in passing—and bolted it firmly.

With a sigh of resignation, Bisnu threw off all his clothes except his underwear and stretched himself out on the earthen floor.

'We will be rid of the beast soon,' said his mother. 'I know it in my heart. Our prayers will be heard, and you shall go to school and pass your exams.'

To cheer up her children, she told them a humorous story which had been handed down to her by her grandmother. It was all about a tiger, a panther and a bear, the three of whom were made to feel very foolish by a thief hiding in the hollow trunk of a banyan tree. Bisnu was sleepy and did not listen very attentively. He dropped off to sleep before the story was finished.

When he woke, it was dark and his mother and sister were asleep on the cot. He wondered what it was that had woken him. He could hear his sister's easy breathing and the steady ticking of the clock. Far away an owl hooted—an unlucky sign, his mother would have said; but she was asleep and Bisnu was not superstitious.

And then he heard something scratching at the door, and the hair on his head felt tight and prickly. It was like a cat scratching, only louder. The door creaked a little whenever it felt the impact of the paw—a heavy paw, as Bisnu could tell from the dull sound it made.

'It's the panther,' he muttered under his breath, sitting up on the hard floor.

The door, he felt, was strong enough to resist the panther's weight. And if he set up an alarm, he could rouse the village. But the middle of the night was no time for the bravest of men to tackle a panther.

In a corner of the room stood a long bamboo stick with a sharp knife tied to one end, which Bisnu sometimes used for spearing fish. Crawling on all fours across the room, he grasped the home-made spear, and then scrambling on to a cupboard, he drew level with the skylight window. He could get his head and shoulders through the window.

'What are you doing up there?' said Puja, who had woken up at the sound of Bisnu shuffling about the room.

'Be quiet,' said Bisnu. 'You'll wake Mother.'

Their mother was awake by now. 'Come down from there, Bisnu. I can hear a noise outside.'

'Don't worry,' said Bisnu, who found himself looking down on the wriggling animal which was trying to get its paw in under the door. With his mother and Puja awake, there was no time to lose. He had got the spear through the window, and though he could not manoeuvre it so as to strike the panther's head, he brought the sharp end down with considerable force on the animal's rump.

With a roar of pain and rage the man-eater leapt down from the steps and disappeared into the darkness. It did not pause to see what had struck it. Certain that no human could have come upon it in that fashion, it ran fearfully to its lair, howling until the pain subsided.

VIII

A panther is an enigma. There are occasions when it proves himself to be the most cunning animal under the sun, and yet the very next day it will walk into an obvious trap that no self-respecting jackal would ever go near. One day a panther will prove itself to be a complete coward and run like a hare from a couple of dogs, and the very next it will dash in amongst half a dozen men sitting round a camp fire and inflict terrible injuries on them.

It is not often that a panther is taken by surprise, as its power of sight and hearing are very acute. It is a master at the art of camouflage, and its spotted coat is admirably suited for the purpose. It does not need heavy jungle to hide in. A couple of bushes and the light and shade from surrounding trees are enough to make it almost invisible.

Because the Manjari panther had been fooled by Bisnu, it did not mean that it was a stupid panther. It simply meant that it had been a little careless. And Bisnu and Puja, growing in confidence since their midnight encounter with the animal, became a little careless themselves.

Puja was hoeing the last field above the house and Bisnu, at the other end of the same field, was chopping up several branches of green oak, prior to leaving the wood to dry in the loft. It was late afternoon and the descending sun glinted in patches on the small river. It was a time of day when only the most desperate and daring of man-eaters would be likely to show itself.

Pausing for a moment to wipe the sweat from his brow, Bisnu glanced up at the hillside, and his eye caught sight of a rock on the brown of the hill which seemed unfamiliar to him. Just as he was about to look elsewhere, the round rock began to grow and then alter its shape, and Bisnu watching in fascination was at last able to make out the head and forequarters of the panther. It looked enormous from the angle at which he saw it, and for a moment he thought it was a tiger. But Bisnu knew instinctively that it was the man-eater.

Slowly, the wary beast pulled itself to its feet and began to walk round the side of the great rock. For a second it disappeared and Bisnu wondered if it had gone away. Then it reappeared and the boy was all excitement again. Very slowly and silently the panther walked across the face of the rock until it was in direct line with the corner of the field where Puja was working.

With a thrill of horror Bisnu realized that the panther was stalking his sister. He shook himself free from the spell which had woven itself round him and shouting hoarsely ran forward.

'Run, Puja, run!' he called. 'It's on the hill above you!'

Puja turned to see what Bisnu was shouting about. She saw him gesticulate to the hill behind her, looked up just in time to see the panther crouching for his spring.

With great presence of mind, she leapt down the banking of the field and tumbled into an irrigation ditch.

The springing panther missed its prey, lost its foothold on the slippery shale banking and somersaulted into the ditch a few feet away from Puja. Before the animal could recover from its surprise, Bisnu was dashing down the slope, swinging his axe and shouting, *'Maro, maro!* (Kill, kill!)'

Two men came running across the field. They, too, were armed with axes. Together with Bisnu they made a half-circle around the snarling animal, which turned at bay and plunged at them in order to get away. Puja wriggled along the ditch on her stomach. The men aimed their axes at the panther's head, and Bisnu had the satisfaction of getting in a well-aimed blow between the eyes. The animal then charged straight at one of the men, knocked him over and tried to get at his throat. Just then Sanjay's father arrived with his long spear. He plunged the end of the spear into the panther's neck.

The panther left its victim and ran into the bushes, dragging the spear through the grass and leaving a trail of blood on the ground. The men followed cautiously—all except the man who had been wounded and who lay on the ground, while Puja and the other womenfolk rushed up to help him.

The panther had made for the bed of the stream and Bisnu, Sanjay's father and their companion were able to follow it quite easily. The water was red where the panther had crossed the stream, and the rocks were stained with blood. After they had gone downstream for about a furlong, they found the panther lying still on its side at the edge of the water. It was mortally wounded, but it continued to wave its tail like an angry cat. Then, even the tail lay still.

'It is dead,' said Bisnu. 'It will not trouble us again in this body.'

'Let us be certain,' said Sanjay's father, and he bent down and pulled the panther's tail.

There was no response.

'It is dead,' said Kalam Singh. 'No panther would suffer such an insult were it alive!'

They cut down a long piece of thick bamboo and tied the panther to it by its feet. Then, with their enemy hanging upside down from the bamboo pole, they started back for the village.

'There will be a feast at my house tonight,' said Kalam Singh. 'Everyone in the village must come. And tomorrow we will visit all the villages in the valley and show them the dead panther, so that they may move about again without fear.'

'We can sell the skin in Kemptee,' said their companion. 'It will fetch a good price.'

'But the claws we will give to Bisnu,' said Kalam Singh, putting his arm around the boy's shoulders. 'He has done a man's work today. He deserves the claws.'

A panther's or tiger's claws are considered to be lucky charms.

'I will take only three claws,' said Bisnu. 'One each for my mother and sister, and one for myself. You may give the others to Sanjay and Chittru and the smaller children.'

As the sun set, a big fire was lit in the middle of the village of Manjari and the people gathered round it, singing and laughing. Kalam Singh killed his fattest goat and there was meat for everyone.

IX

Bisnu was on his way home. He had just handed in his first paper, arithmetic, which he had found quite easy. Tomorrow it would be algebra, and when he got home he would have to practice square roots and cube roots and fractional coefficients.

Mr Nautiyal and the entire class had been happy that he had been able to sit for the exams. He was also a hero to them for his part in killing the panther. The story had spread through the villages with the rapidity of a forest fire, a fire which was now raging in Kemptee town.

When he walked past the hospital, he was whistling cheerfully. Dr Taylor waved to him from the verandah steps.

'How is Sanjay now?' she asked.

'He is well,' said Bisnu.

'And your mother and sister?'

'They are well,' said Bisnu.

'Are you going to get yourself a new dog?'

'I am thinking about it,' said Bisnu. 'At present I have a baby goat—I am teaching it to swim!'

He started down the path to the valley. Dark clouds had gathered and there was a rumble of thunder. A storm was imminent.

'Wait for me!' shouted Sarru, running down the path behind Bisnu, his milk pails clanging against each other. He fell into step beside Bisnu.

'Well, I hope we don't have any more man-eaters for some time,' he said. 'I've lost a lot of money by not being able to take milk up to Kemptee.'

'We should be safe as long as a shikari doesn't wound another panther. There was an old bullet wound in the man-eater's thigh. That's why it couldn't hunt in the forest. The deer were too fast for it.'

'Is there a new postman yet?'

'He starts tomorrow. A cousin of Mela Ram's.'

When they reached the parting of their ways it had begun to rain a little.

'I must hurry,' said Sarru. 'It's going to get heavier any minute.'

'I feel like getting wet,' said Bisnu. 'This time it's the monsoon, I'm sure.'

Bisnu entered the forest on his own, and at the same time the rain came down in heavy opaque sheets. The trees shook in the wind, the langurs chattered with excitement.

It was still pouring when Bisnu emerged from the forest, drenched to the skin. But the rain stopped suddenly, just as the village of Manjari came in view. The sun appeared through a rift in the clouds. The leaves and the grass gave out a sweet, fresh smell.

Bisnu could see his mother and sister in the field transplanting the rice seedlings. The menfolk were driving the yoked oxen through the thin mud of the fields, while the children hung on to the oxen's tails, standing on the plain wooden harrows and with weird cries and shouts sending the animals almost at a gallop along the narrow terraces.

Bisnu felt the urge to be with them, working in the fields. He ran down the path, his feet falling softly on the wet earth. Puja saw him coming and waved to him. She met him at the edge of the field.

'How did you find your paper today?' she asked.

'Oh, it was easy.' Bisnu slipped his hand into hers and together they walked across the field. Puja felt something smooth and hard against her fingers, and before she could see what Bisnu was doing, he had slipped a pair of bangles over her wrist.

'I remembered,' he said, with a sense of achievement. Puja looked at the bangles and burst out: 'But they are blue, Bhai, and I wanted red and gold bangles!' And then, when she saw him looking crestfallen, she hurried on: 'But they are very pretty, and you did remember... Actually, they're just as nice as red and gold bangles! Come into the house when you are ready. I have made something special for you.'

'I am coming,' said Bisnu, turning towards the house. 'You don't know how hungry a man gets, walking five miles to reach home!'

COPPERFIELD IN THE JUNGLE

Grandfather never hunted wild animals; he could not understand the pleasure some people obtained from killing the creatures of our forests. Birds and animals, he felt, had as much right to live as humans. There was some justification in killing for food—most animals did—but none at all in killing just for the fun of it.

At the age of twelve, I did not have the same high principles as Grandfather. Nevertheless, I disliked anything to do with shikar or hunting. I found it terribly boring.

Uncle Henry and some of his sporting friends once took me on a shikar expedition into the Terai forests of the Siwaliks. The prospect of a whole week in the jungle as camp follower to several adults with guns filled me with dismay. I knew that long, weary hours would be spent tramping behind these tall, professional-looking huntsmen. They could only speak in terms of bagging this tiger or that wild elephant, when all they ever got, if they were lucky, was a wild hare or a partridge. Tigers and excitement, it seemed, came only to Jim Corbett.

This particular expedition proved to be different from others. There were four men with guns, and at the end of the week, all that they had shot were two miserable, underweight wild fowls. But I managed, on our second day in the jungle, to be left behind at the rest house. And, in the course of a morning's exploration of the old bungalow, I discovered a shelf of books half-hidden in a corner of the back verandah.

Who had left them there? A literary forest officer? A memsahib who had been bored by her husband's camp-fire boasting? Or someone who had no interest in the 'manly' sport of slaughtering wild animals and had brought his library along to pass the time?

Or possibly the poor fellow had gone into the jungle one day, as a gesture towards his more bloodthirsty companions, and been trampled by an elephant, or gored by a wild boar, or (more likely) accidentally shot by one of the shikaris and his sorrowing friends had taken his remains away and left his books behind.

Anyway, there they were—a shelf of some thirty volumes, obviously untouched for many years. I wiped the thick dust off the covers and examined the titles. As my reading tastes had not yet formed, I was willing to try anything. The bookshelf was varied in its contents—and my own interests have since remained fairly universal.

On that fateful day in the forest rest house, I discovered P.G. Wodehouse and read his *Love Among the Chickens*, an early Ukridge story and still one of my favourites. By the time the perspiring hunters came home late in the evening, with their spent cartridges and lame excuses, I had made a start with M.R. James's *Ghost Stories of an Antiquary*, which had me hooked on ghost stories for the rest of my life. It kept me awake most of the night, until the oil in the kerosene lamp had finished.

Next morning, fresh and optimistic again, the shikaris set out for a different area, where they hoped to 'bag a tiger'. They had employed a party of villagers to beat the jungle, and all day I could hear their drums throbbing in the distance. This did not prevent me from finishing M.R. James or discovering a book called *A Naturalist on the Prowl* by Edward Hamilton Aitken.

My concentration was disturbed only once, when I looked up and saw a spotted deer crossing the open clearing in front of the bungalow. The deer disappeared among the sal trees, and I returned to my book.

Dusk had fallen when I heard the party returning from the hunt. The great men were talking loudly and seemed excited. Perhaps they had got their tiger. I put down my book and came out to meet them.

'Did you shoot the tiger?' I asked excitedly.

'No, my boy,' said Uncle Henry. 'I think we'll bag it tomorrow. But you should have been with us—we saw a spotted deer!'

◆

There were three days left and I knew I would never get through the entire bookshelf. So I chose *David Copperfield*—my first encounter with Dickens—and settled down on the verandah armchair to make the acquaintance of Mr Micawber and his family, Aunt Betsy Trotwood, Mr Dick, Peggotty, and a host of other larger-than-life people. I think it would be true to say that *David Copperfield* set me off on the road to literature; I identified with young David and wanted to grow up to be a writer like him.

But on my second day with the book, an event occurred which disturbed my reading for a little while.

I had noticed, on the previous day, that a number of stray dogs—belonging to watchmen, villagers and forest guards—always hung about the house, waiting for scraps of food to be thrown away. It was ten o'clock in the morning, a time when wild animals seldom come into the open, when I heard a sudden yelp in the clearing. Looking up, I saw a large leopard making off into the jungle with one of the dogs held in its jaws. The leopard had either been driven towards the house by the beaters, or had watched the party leave the bungalow and decided to help itself to a meal.

There was no one else about at the time. Since the dog

was obviously dead within seconds of being seized, and the leopard had disappeared, I saw no point in raising an alarm which would have interrupted my reading. So I returned to *David Copperfield*.

It was getting late when the shikaris returned. They were dirty, sweaty and as usual, disappointed. Next day we were to return to the city, and none of the hunters had anything to show for a week in the jungle. Swear words punctuated their conversation.

'No game left in these… jungles,' said the leading member of the party, famed for once having shot two man-eating tigers and a basking crocodile in rapid succession.

'It's this beastly weather,' said Uncle Henry. 'No rain for months.'

'I saw a leopard this morning,' I said modestly.

But no one took me seriously. 'Did you really?' said the leading hunter, glancing at the book beside me. 'Young Master Copperfield says he saw a leopard!'

'Too imaginative for his age,' said Uncle Henry. 'Comes from reading too much, I suppose.'

'If you were to get out of the house and into the jungle,' said the third member, 'you might really see a leopard! Don't know what young chaps are coming to these days.'

I went to bed early and left them to their tales of the 'good old days' when rhinos, cheetahs and possibly even the legendary phoenix were still available for slaughter.

Next day the camp broke up and we went our different ways. I was still only half-way through *David Copperfield*, but I saw no reason why it should be left behind to gather dust for another thirty years, and so I took it home with me. I have it still, a reminder of how I failed as a shikari but launched myself on a literary career.

THE ELEPHANT AND THE
CASSOWARY BIRD

The baby elephant wasn't out of place in our home in north India because India is where elephants belong, and in any case, our house was full of pets brought home by Grandfather, who was in the Forest Service. But the cassowary bird was different. No one had seen such a bird before—not in India, that is. Grandfather had picked it up on a voyage to Singapore, where he'd been given the bird by a rubber planter who'd got it from a Dutch trader who'd got it from a man in Indonesia.

Anyway, it ended up at our home in Dehra, and seemed to do quite well in the subtropical climate. It looked like a cross between a turkey and an ostrich, but bigger than the former and smaller than the latter—about five feet in height. It was not a beautiful bird, nor even a friendly one, but it had come to stay, and everyone was curious about it, especially the baby elephant.

Right from the start, the baby elephant took a great interest in the cassowary, a bird unlike any found in the Indian jungles. He would circle round the odd creature, and diffidently examine with his trunk the texture of its stumpy wings. Of course he suspected no evil, and his childlike curiosity encouraged him to take liberties, which resulted in an unpleasant experience.

Noticing the baby elephant's attempts to make friends with the rather morose cassowary, we felt a bit apprehensive. Self-contained and sullen, the big bird responded only by slowly and slyly raising one of its powerful legs, in the meantime gazing into space with an innocent air. We knew what the gesture meant;

we had seen that treacherous leg raised on many an occasion, and suddenly shooting out with a force that would have done credit to a vicious camel. In fact, camel and cassowary kicks are delivered on the same plan, except that the camel kicks backward like a horse and the bird forward.

We wished to spare our baby elephant a painful experience, and led him away from the bird. But he persisted in his friendly overtures, and one morning, he received an ugly reward. Rapid as lightning, the cassowary hit straight from the hip and knee joints, and the elephant ran squealing to Grandfather.

For several days he avoided the cassowary, and we thought he had learnt his lesson. He crossed and recrossed the compound and the garden, swinging his trunk, thinking furiously. Then, a week later, he appeared on the verandah at breakfast time in his usual cheery, childlike fashion, sidling up to the cassowary as if nothing had happened.

We were struck with amazement at this and so, it seemed, was the bird. Had the painful lesson already been forgotten, and by a member of the elephant tribe noted for its ability to never forget? Another dose of the same medicine would serve the booby right.

The cassowary once more began to draw up its fighting leg with sinister determination. It was nearing the true position for the master kick, kung fu style, when all of a sudden the baby elephant seized with his trunk the cassowary's other leg and pulled it down. There was a clumsy flapping of wings, a tremendous swelling of the bird's wattle, and an undignified getting up, as if it were a floored boxer doing his best to beat the count of ten. The bird then marched off with an attempt to look stately and unconcerned, while we at the breakfast table were convulsed with laughter.

After this, the cassowary bird gave the baby elephant as

wide a berth as possible. But they were not forced to coexist for very long. The baby elephant, getting bulky and cumbersome, was sold and now lives in a zoo where he is a favourite with young visitors who love to take rides on his back.

As for the cassowary, he continued to grace our verandah for many years, gaped at but not made much of, while entering on a rather friendless old age.

THE EYES OF THE EAGLE

It was a high, piercing sound, almost like the yelping of a dog. Jai stopped picking the wild strawberries that grew in the grass around him, and looked up at the sky. He had a dog—a shaggy guard-dog called Motu—but Motu did not yet yelp, he growled and barked. The strange sound came from the sky, and Jai had heard it before. Now, realizing what it was, he jumped to his feet, calling to his dog, calling his sheep to start for home. Motu came bounding towards him, ready for a game.

'Not now, Motu!' said Jai. 'We must get the lambs home quickly.' Again he looked up at the sky.

He saw it now, a black speck against the sun, growing larger as it circled the mountain, coming lower every moment—a golden eagle, king of the skies over the higher Himalayas, ready now to swoop and seize its prey.

Had it seen a pheasant or a pine marten? Or was it after one of the lambs? Jai had never lost a lamb to an eagle, but recently some of the other shepherds had been talking about a golden eagle that had been preying on their flocks.

The sheep had wandered some way down the side of the mountain, and Jai ran after them to make sure that none of the lambs had gone off on its own.

Motu ran about, barking furiously. He wasn't very good at keeping the sheep together—he was often bumping into them and sending them tumbling down the slope—but his size and bear-like look kept the leopards and wolves at a distance.

Jai was counting the lambs; they were bleating loudly and staying close to their mothers. *One—two—three—four...*

There should have been a fifth. Jai couldn't see it on the slope below him. He looked up towards a rocky ledge near the steep path to the Tung temple. The golden eagle was circling the rocks.

The bird disappeared from sight for a moment, then rose again with a small creature grasped firmly in its terrible talons.

'It has taken a lamb!' shouted Jai. He started scrambling up the slope. Motu ran ahead of him, barking furiously at the big bird as it glided away, over the tops of the stunted junipers to its eyrie on the cliffs above Tung.

There was nothing that Jai and Motu could do except stare helplessly and angrily at the disappearing eagle. The lamb had died the instant it had been struck. The rest of the flock seemed unaware of what had happened. They still grazed on the thick, sweet grass of the mountain slopes.

'We had better drive them home, Motu,' said Jai, and at a nod from the boy, the big dog bounded down the slope, to take part in his favourite game of driving the sheep homewards. Soon he had them running all over the place, and Jai had to dash about trying to keep them together. Finally, they straggled homewards.

'A fine lamb gone,' said Jai to himself gloomily. 'I wonder what Grandfather will say.'

Grandfather said, 'Never mind. It had to happen some day. That eagle has been watching the sheep for some time.'

Grandmother, more practical, said: 'We could have sold the lamb for three hundred rupees. You'll have to be more careful in future, Jai. Don't fall asleep on the hillside, and don't read story-books when you are supposed to be watching the sheep!'

'I wasn't reading this morning,' said Jai truthfully, forgetting to mention that he had been gathering strawberries.

'It's good for him to read,' said Grandfather, who had never had the luck to go to school. In his days, there weren't any schools in the mountains. Now there was one in every village.

'Time enough to read at night,' said Grandmother, who did not think much of the little one-room school down at Maku, their home village.

'Well, these are the October holidays,' said Grandfather. 'Otherwise he would not be here to help us with the sheep. It will snow by the end of the month, and then we will move with the flock. You will have more time for reading then, Jai.'

At Maku, which was down in the warmer valley, Jai's parents tilled a few narrow terraces on which they grew barley, millets and potatoes. The old people brought their sheep up to the Tung meadows to graze during the summer months. They stayed in a small stone hut just off the path that pilgrims took to the ancient temple. At 12,000 feet above sea level, it was the highest Hindu temple on the inner Himalayan ranges.

The following day Jai and Motu were very careful. They did not let the sheep out of sight even for a minute. Nor did they catch sight of the golden eagle. 'What if it attacks again?' wondered Jai. 'How will I stop it?'

The great eagle, with its powerful beak and talons, was more than a match for boy or dog. Its hind claw, four inches round the curve, was its most dangerous weapon. When it spread its wings, the distance from tip to tip was more than eight feet.

The eagle did not come that day because it had fed well and was now resting in its eyrie. Old bones, which had belonged to pheasants, snow-cocks, pine martens and even foxes, were scattered about the rocks that formed the eagle's home. The eagle had a mate, but it was not the breeding season and she was away on a scouting expedition of her own.

The golden eagle stood on its rocky ledge, staring majestically across the valley. Its hard, unblinking eyes missed nothing. Those strange orange-yellow eyes could spot a field rat or a mouse hare more than a hundred yards below.

There were other eagles on the mountain, but usually they kept to their own territory. And only the bolder ones went for lambs, because the flocks were always protected by men and dogs.

The eagle took off from its eyrie and glided gracefully, powerfully over the valley, circling the Tung mountain.

Below lay the old temple, built from slabs of grey granite. A line of pilgrims snaked up the steep, narrow path. On the meadows below the peak, the sheep grazed peacefully, unaware of the presence of the eagle. The great bird's shadow slid over the sunlit slopes.

The eagle saw the boy and the dog, but he did not fear them. He had his eye on a lamb that was frisking about on the grass, a few feet away from the other grazing sheep.

Jai did not see the eagle until it swept round an outcrop of rocks about a hundred feet away. It moved silently, without any movement of its wings, for it had already built up the momentum for its dive. Now it came straight at the lamb.

Motu saw the bird in time. With a low growl he dashed forward and reached the side of the lamb at almost the same instant that the eagle swept in.

There was a terrific collision. Feathers flew. The eagle screamed with rage. The lamb tumbled down the slope, and Motu howled in pain as the huge beak struck him high on the leg.

The big bird, a little stunned by the clash, flew off rather unsteadily, with a mighty beating of its wings.

Motu had saved the lamb. It was frightened but unhurt. Bleating loudly, it joined the other sheep, who took up the bleating. Jai ran up to Motu, who lay whimpering on the ground. There was no sign of the eagle. Quickly he removed his shirt and vest; then he wrapped his vest round the dog's wound, tying it in position with his belt.

Motu could not get up, and he was much too heavy for Jai to carry. Jai did not want to leave his dog alone, in case the eagle returned to attack.

He stood up, cupped his hand to his mouth, and began calling for his grandfather.

'Dada, dada!' he shouted, and presently Grandfather heard him and came stumbling down the slope. He was followed by another shepherd, and together they lifted Motu and carried him home.

Motu had a bad wound, but Grandmother cleaned it and applied a paste made of herbs. Then she laid strips of carrot over the wound—an old mountain remedy—and bandaged the leg. But it would be some time before Motu could run about again. By then it would probably be snowing and time to leave these high-altitude pastures and return to the valley. Meanwhile, the sheep had to be taken out to graze, and Grandfather decided to accompany Jai for the remaining period.

They did not see the golden eagle for two or three days, and, when they did, it was flying over the next range. Perhaps it had found some other source of food, or even another flock of sheep. 'Are you afraid of the eagle?' Grandfather asked Jai.

'I wasn't before,' said Jai. 'Not until it hurt Motu. I did not know it could be so dangerous. But Motu hurt it too. He banged straight into it!'

'Perhaps it won't bother us again,' said Grandfather thoughtfully. 'A bird's wing is easily injured—even an eagle's.'

Jai wasn't so sure. He had seen it strike twice, and he knew that it was not afraid of anyone. Only when it learnt to fear his presence would it keep away from the flock.

The next day Grandfather did not feel well; he was feverish

and kept to his bed. Motu was hobbling about gamely on three legs; the wounded leg was still very sore.

'Don't go too far with the sheep,' said Grandmother. 'Let them graze near the house.'

'But there's hardly any grass here,' said Jai.

'I don't want you wandering off while that eagle is still around.'

'Give him my stick,' said Grandfather from his bed. Grandmother took it from the corner and handed it to the boy.

It was an old stick, made of wild cherry wood, which Grandfather often carried around. The wood was strong and well-seasoned; the stick was stout and long. It reached up to Jai's shoulders.

'Don't lose it,' said Grandfather. 'It was given to me many years ago by a wandering scholar who came to the Tung temple. I was going to give it to you when you got bigger, but perhaps this is the right time for you to have it. If the eagle comes near you, swing the stick around your head. That should frighten it off!'

Clouds had gathered over the mountains, and a heavy mist hid the Tung temple. With the approach of winter, the flow of pilgrims had been reduced to a trickle. The shepherds had started leaving the lush meadows and returning to their villages at lower altitudes. Very soon, the bears and the leopards and the golden eagles would have the high ranges all to themselves.

Jai used the cherry wood stick to prod the sheep along the path until they reached the steep meadows. The stick would have to be a substitute for Motu. And they seemed to respond to it more readily than they did to Motu's mad charges.

Because of the sudden cold and the prospect of snow, Grandmother had made Jai wear a rough woollen jacket and a pair of high boots bought from a Tibetan trader. He wasn't used to the boots—he wore sandals at other times—and had some difficulty in climbing quickly up and down the hillside. It was tiring work, trying to keep the flock together. The cawing of some crows warned Jai that the eagle might be around, but the mist prevented him from seeing very far.

After some time the mist lifted and Jai was able to see the temple and the snow-peaks towering behind it. He saw the golden eagle, too. It was circling high overhead. Jai kept close to the flock—one eye on the eagle, one eye on the restless sheep.

Then the great bird stooped and flew lower. It circled the temple and then pretended to go away. Jai felt sure it would be back. And a few minutes later, it reappeared from the other side of the mountain. It was much lower now, wings spread out and back, taloned feet to the fore, piercing eyes fixed on its target—a small lamb that had suddenly gone frisking down the slope, away from Jai and the flock.

Now it flew lower still, only a few feet off the ground, paying no attention to the boy.

It passed Jai with a great rush of air, and, as it did so, the boy struck out with his stick and caught the bird a glancing blow.

The eagle missed its prey, and the tiny lamb skipped away.

To Jai's amazement, the bird did not fly off. Instead it landed on the hillside and glared at the boy, as a king would glare at a humble subject who had dared to pelt him with a pebble.

The golden eagle stood almost as tall as Jai. Its wings were still outspread. Its fierce eyes seemed to be looking through and through the boy.

Jai's first instinct was to turn and run. But the cherry wood stick was still in his hands, and he felt sure there was power in it. He saw that the eagle was about to launch itself again at the lamb. Instead of running away, he ran forward, the stick raised above his head.

The eagle rose a few feet off the ground and struck out with its huge claws.

Luckily for Jai, his heavy jacket took the force of the blow. A talon ripped through the sleeve, and the sleeve fell away. At the same time the heavy stick caught the eagle across its open wing. The bird gave a shrill cry of pain and fury. Then it turned and flapped heavily away, flying unsteadily because of its injured wing.

Jai still clutched the stick, because he expected the bird to return; he did not even glance at his torn jacket. But the golden eagle had alighted on a distant rock and was in no hurry to return to the attack.

Jai began driving the sheep home. The clouds had become heavy and black, and presently the first snow-flakes began to fall.

Jai saw a hare go lolloping down the hill. When it was about fifty yards away, there was a rush of air from the eagle's beating wings, and Jai saw the bird approaching the hare in a sidelong drive.

'So it hasn't been badly hurt,' thought Jai, feeling a little relieved, for he could not help admiring the great bird. 'Now it has found something else to chase for its dinner.'

The hare saw the eagle and dodged about, making for a clump of junipers. Jai did not know if it was caught or not, because the snow and sleet had increased and both bird and hare were lost in the gathering snow-storm.

The sheep were bleating behind him. One of the lambs looked tired, and he stooped to pick it up. As he did so, he heard a thin, whining sound. It grew louder by the second. Before he could look up, a huge wing caught him across the shoulders and sent him sprawling. The lamb tumbled down the slope with him, into a thorny bilberry bush.

The bush saved them. Jai saw the eagle coming in again, flying low. It was another eagle! One had been vanquished, and now here was another, just as big and fearless, probably the mate of the first eagle.

Jai had lost his stick and there was no way by which he could fight the second eagle. So he crept further into the bush, holding the lamb beneath him. At the same time he began shouting at the top of his voice—both to scare the bird away and to summon help. The eagle could not easily get at them now; but the rest of the flock was exposed on the hillside. Surely the eagle would make for them.

Even as the bird circled and came back in another dive, Jai heard fierce barking. The eagle immediately swung away and rose skywards.

The barking came from Motu. Hearing Jai's shouts and sensing that something was wrong, he had come limping out of the house, ready to do battle. Behind him came another shepherd and—most wonderful of all—Grandmother herself, banging two frying-pans together. The barking, the banging and the shouting frightened the eagles away. The sheep scattered too, and it was some time before they could all be rounded up. By then it was snowing heavily.

'Tomorrow we must all go down to Maku,' said the shepherd.

'Yes, it's time we went,' said Grandmother. 'You can read your story-books again, Jai.'

'I'll have my own story to tell,' said Jai.

When they reached the hut and Jai saw Grandfather, he said, 'Oh, I've forgotten your stick!'

But Motu had picked it up. Carrying it between his teeth, he brought it home and sat down with it in the open doorway. He had decided the cherry wood was good for his teeth and would have chewed it up if Grandmother hadn't taken it from him.

'Never mind,' said Grandfather, sitting up on his cot. 'It isn't the stick that matters. It's the person who holds it.'

THE SONG OF THE
WHISTLING THRUSH

In the wooded hills of western India lives 'The Idle Schoolboy'—a bird who cannot learn a simple tune, though he is gifted with one of the most beautiful voices in the forest. He whistles away in various sharps and flats, and sometimes, when you think he is really going to produce a melody, he breaks off in the middle of his song as though he had just remembered something very important.

Why is it that the Whistling Thrush can never remember a tune? The story goes that on a hot summer's afternoon, the young God Krishna was wandering along the banks of a mountain stream when he came to a small waterfall, shot through with sunbeams. It was a lovely spot, cool and inviting. Tiny fish flecked the pool at the foot of the waterfall, and a Paradise Flycatcher, trailing its silver tail, moved gracefully amongst the trees.

Krishna was enchanted. He threw himself down on a bed of moss and ferns, and began playing on his flute—the famous flute with which he had charmed all the creatures in the forest. A fat yellow lizard nodded its head in time to the music; the birds were hushed; and the shy mouse-deer approached silently on their tiny hooves to see who it was who played so beautifully.

Presently the flute slipped from Krishna's fingers, and the beautiful young god fell asleep. But it was not a restful sleep, for his dreams were punctuated by an annoying whistling, as though someone who didn't know much about music was practising on his flute in an attempt to learn the tune that Krishna had been playing.

Awake now, Krishna sat up and saw a ragged urchin standing ankle-deep in the pool, the sacred flute held to his lips!

Krishna was furious.

'Come here, boy!' he shouted. 'How dare you steal my flute and disturb my sleep! Don't you know who I am?'

The boy, instead of being afraid, was thrilled at the discovery that he stood before his hero, the young Krishna, whose exploits were famous throughout the land.

'I did not steal your flute, lord,' he said. 'Had that been my intention, I would not have waited for you to wake up. It was only my great love for your music that made me touch your flute. You will teach me to play, will you not? I will be your disciple.'

Krishna's anger melted away, and he was filled with compassion for the boy. But it was too late to do anything, for it is everlastingly decreed that anyone who touches the sacred property of the gods, whether deliberately or in innocence, must be made to suffer throughout his next ten thousand births.

When this was explained to the boy, he fell on his face and wept bitterly, crying, 'Have mercy on me, Krishna. Do with me as you will, but do not send me away from the beautiful forests I love.'

Swiftly, Krishna communed in spirit with Brahma the Creator. Here was a genuine case of a crime committed in ignorance. If it could not be forgiven, surely the punishment could be less severe?

Brahma agreed, and Krishna laid his hand on the boy's mouth, saying, 'For ever try to copy the song of the gods, but never succeed.' Then he touched the boy's clothes and said, 'Let the raggedness and dust disappear, and only the beautiful colours of Krishna remain.'

Immediately the boy was changed into the bird we know today as the Whistling Thrush of Malabar, with its dark body and brilliant blue patches on head and wings. In this guise, he still continues to live among the beautiful, forested valleys of the hills, where he tries unsuccessfully to remember the tune that brought about his strange transformation.

A TIGER IN THE HOUSE

Timothy, the tiger cub, was discovered by Grandfather on a hunting expedition in the Terai jungle near Dehra.

Grandfather was no shikari, but as he knew the forests of the Siwalik hills better than most people, he was persuaded to accompany the party—it consisted of several Very Important Persons from Delhi—to advise on the terrain and the direction the beaters should take once a tiger had been spotted.

The camp itself was sumptuous—seven large tents (one for each shikari), a dining tent and a number of servants' tents. The dinner was very good, as Grandfather admitted afterwards; it was not often that one saw hot-water plates, finger glasses and seven or eight courses in a tent in the jungle! But that was how things were done in the days of the viceroys... There were also some fifteen elephants, four of them with howdahs for the shikaris, and the others specially trained for taking part in the beat.

The sportsmen never saw a tiger, nor did they shoot anything else, though they saw a number of deer, peacock and wild boar. They were giving up all hope of finding a tiger and were beginning to shoot at jackals, when Grandfather, strolling down the forest path at some distance from the rest of the party, discovered a little tiger about eighteen inches long, hiding among the intricate roots of a banyan tree. Grandfather picked him up and brought him home after the camp had broken up. He had the distinction of being the only member of the party to have bagged any game, dead or alive.

At first the tiger cub, who was named Timothy by Grandmother, was brought up entirely on milk given to him in a feeding bottle by our cook, Mahmoud. But the milk proved too rich for him, and he was put on a diet of raw mutton and cod liver oil, to be followed later by a more tempting diet of pigeons and rabbits.

Timothy was provided with two companions—Toto the monkey, who was bold enough to pull the young tiger by the tail, and then climb up the curtains if Timothy lost his temper; and a small mongrel puppy, found on the road by Grandfather.

At first Timothy appeared to be quite afraid of the puppy and darted back with a spring if it came too near. He would make absurd dashes at it with his large forepaws and then retreat to a ridiculously safe distance. Finally, he allowed the puppy to crawl on his back and rest there!

One of Timothy's favourite amusements was to stalk anyone who would play with him, and so, when I came to live with Grandfather, I became one of the tiger's favourites. With a crafty look in his glittering eyes, and his body crouching, he would creep closer and closer to me, suddenly making a dash for my feet, rolling over on his back and kicking with delight, and pretending to bite my ankles.

He was by this time the size of a full-grown retriever, and when I took him out for walks, people on the road would give us a wide berth. When he pulled hard on his chain, I had difficulty in keeping up with him. His favourite place in the house was the drawing room, and he would make himself comfortable on the long sofa, reclining there with great dignity and snarling at anybody who tried to get him off.

Timothy had clean habits, and would scrub his face with his paws exactly like a cat. At night, he slept in the cook's quarters and was always delighted at being let out by him in the morning.

'One of these days,' declared Grandmother in her prophetic manner, 'we are going to find Timothy sitting on Mahmoud's bed, and no sign of the cook except his clothes and shoes!'

Of course, it never came to that, but when Timothy was about six months old a change came over him; he grew steadily less friendly. When out for a walk with me, he would try to steal away to stalk a cat or someone's pet Pekingese. Sometimes at night we would hear frenzied cackling from the poultry house, and in the morning there would be feathers lying all over the verandah. Timothy had to be chained up more often. And, finally, when he began to stalk Mahmoud about the house with what looked like villainous intent, Grandfather decided it was time to transfer him to a zoo.

The nearest zoo was at Lucknow, two hundred miles away. Reserving a first-class compartment for himself and Timothy—no one would share a compartment with them—Grandfather took him to Lucknow where the zoo authorities were only too glad to receive as a gift a well-fed and fairly civilized tiger.

About six months later, when my grandparents were visiting relatives in Lucknow, Grandfather took the opportunity of calling at the zoo to see how Timothy was getting on. I was not there to accompany him, but I heard all about it when he returned to Dehra.

Arriving at the zoo, Grandfather made straight for the particular cage in which Timothy had been interned. The tiger was there, crouched in a corner, full-grown and with a magnificent striped coat.

'Hello, Timothy!' said Grandfather and, climbing the railing with ease, he put his arm through the bars of the cage.

The tiger approached the bars and allowed Grandfather to put both hands around his head. Grandfather stroked the tiger's forehead and tickled his ear, and, whenever he growled, smacked him across the mouth, which was his old way of keeping him quiet.

He licked Grandfather's hands and only sprang away when a leopard in the next cage snarled at him. Grandfather 'shooed' the leopard away and the tiger returned to lick his hands; but every now and then the leopard would rush at the bars and the tiger would slink back to his corner.

A number of people had gathered to watch the reunion when a keeper pushed his way through the crowd and asked Grandfather what he was doing.

'I'm talking to Timothy,' said Grandfather. 'Weren't you here when I gave him to the zoo six months ago?'

'I haven't been here very long,' said the surprised keeper. 'Please continue your conversation. But I have never been able to touch him myself, he is always very bad tempered.'

'Why don't you put him somewhere else?' suggested Grandfather. 'That leopard keeps frightening him. I'll go and see the superintendent about it.'

Grandfather went in search of the superintendent of the zoo, but found that he had gone home early; and so, after wandering about the zoo for a little while, he returned to Timothy's cage to say goodbye. It was beginning to get dark.

He had been stroking and slapping Timothy for about five minutes when he found another keeper observing him with some alarm. Grandfather recognized him as the keeper who had been there when Timothy had first come to the zoo.

'*You* remember me,' said Grandfather. 'Now why don't you transfer Timothy to another cage, away from this stupid leopard?'

'But—sir—' stammered the keeper, 'it is not your tiger.'

'I know, I know,' said Grandfather testily. 'I realize he is no longer mine. But you might at least take a suggestion or two from me.'

'I remember your tiger very well,' said the keeper. 'He died two months ago.'

'Died!' exclaimed Grandfather.

'Yes, sir, of pneumonia. This tiger was trapped in the hills only last month, and he is very dangerous!'

Grandfather could think of nothing to say. The tiger was still licking his arm, with increasing relish. Grandfather took what seemed to him an age to withdraw his hand from the cage.

With his face near the tiger's he mumbled, 'Goodnight, Timothy,' and giving the keeper a scornful look, walked briskly out of the zoo.

ROMI AND THE WILDFIRE

1

As Romi was about to mount his bicycle, he saw smoke rising from behind the distant line of trees.

'It looks like a forest fire,' said Prem, his friend and classmate.

'It's well to the east,' said Romi. 'Nowhere near the road.'

'There's a strong wind,' said Prem, looking at the dry leaves swirling across the road.

It was the middle of May, and it hadn't rained in the Terai for several weeks. The grass was brown, the leaves of the trees covered with dust. Even though it was getting on to six o'clock in the evening, the boys' shirts were damp with sweat.

'It will be getting dark soon,' said Prem. 'You'd better spend the night at my house.'

'No, I said I'd be home tonight. My father isn't keeping well. The doctor has given me some tablets for him.'

'You'd better hurry, then. That fire seems to be spreading.'

'Oh, it's far off. It will take me only forty minutes to ride through the forest. Bye, Prem—see you tomorrow!'

Romi mounted his bicycle and pedalled off down the main road of the village, scattering stray hens, stray dogs and stray villagers.

'Hey, look where you're going!' shouted an angry villager, leaping out of the way of the oncoming bicycle. 'Do you think you own the road?'

'Of course I own it,' called Romi cheerfully, and cycled on.

His own village lay about seven miles distant, on the other

side of the forest; but there was only a primary school in his village, and Romi was now in High School. His father, who was a fairly wealthy sugarcane farmer, had only recently bought him the bicycle. Romi didn't care too much for school and felt there weren't enough holidays; but he enjoyed the long rides, and he got on well with his classmates.

He might have stayed the night with Prem had it not been for the tablets which the *Vaid*—the village doctor—had given him for his father.

Romi's father was having back trouble, and the medicine had been specially prepared from local herbs.

Having been given such a fine bicycle, Romi felt that the least he could do in return was to get those tablets to his father as early as possible.

He put his head down and rode swiftly out of the village. Ahead of him, the smoke rose from the burning forest and the sky glowed red.

2

He had soon left the village far behind. There was a slight climb, and Romi had to push harder on the pedals to get over the rise. Once over the top, the road went winding down to the edge of the sub-tropical forest.

This was the part Romi enjoyed most. He relaxed, stopped pedalling, and allowed the bicycle to glide gently down the slope. Soon the wind was rushing past him, blowing his hair about his face and making his shirt billow out behind. He burst into song.

A dog from the village ran beside him, barking furiously. Romi shouted at the dog, encouraging him in the race.

Then the road straightened out, and Romi began pedalling again. The dog, seeing the forest ahead, turned back to the village. It was afraid of the forest.

The smoke was thicker now, and Romi caught the smell of burning timber. But ahead of him, the road was clear. He rode on.

It was a rough, dusty road, cut straight through the forest. Tall trees grew on either side, cutting off the last of the daylight. But the spreading glow of the fire on the right lit up the road, and giant tree-shadows danced before the boy on the bicycle.

Usually the road was deserted. This evening it was alive with wild creatures fleeing from the forest fire.

The first animal that Romi saw was a hare, leaping across the road in front of him. It was followed by several more hares. Then a band of monkeys streamed across, chattering excitedly.

They'll be safe on the other side, thought Romi. *The fire won't cross the road.*

But it was coming closer. And realizing this, Romi pedalled harder. In half-an-hour he should be out of the forest.

Suddenly, from the side of the road, several pheasants rose in the air, and with a *whoosh*, flew low across the path, just in front of the oncoming bicycle. Taken by surprise, Romi fell off. When he picked himself up and began brushing his clothes, he saw that his knee was bleeding. It wasn't a deep cut, but he allowed it to bleed a little, took out his handkerchief and bandaged his knee. Then he mounted the bicycle again.

He rode a bit slower now, because birds and animals kept coming out of the bushes.

Not only pheasants but smaller birds, too, were streaming across the road—parrots, jungle crows, owls, magpies—and the air was filled with their cries.

Everyone's on the move, thought Romi. *It must be a really big fire.*

He could see the flames now, reaching out from behind the trees on his right, and he could hear the crackling as the dry leaves caught fire. The air was hot on his face. Leaves, still alight or turning to cinders, floated past.

A herd of deer crossed the road, and Romi had to stop until they had passed. Then he mounted again and rode on; but now, for the first time, he was feeling afraid.

3

From ahead came a faint clanging sound. It wasn't an animal sound, Romi was sure of that. A fire-engine? There were no fire-engines within fifty miles.

The clanging came nearer, and Romi discovered that the noise came from a small boy who was running along the forest path, two milk-cans clattering at his side.

'Teju!' called Romi, recognizing the boy from a neighbouring village. 'What are you doing out here?'

'Trying to get home, of course,' said Teju, panting along beside the bicycle.

'Jump on,' said Romi, stopping for him.

Teju was only eight or nine—a couple of years younger than Romi. He had come to deliver milk to some road-workers, but the workers had left at the first signs of the fire, and Teju was hurrying home with his cans still full of milk.

He got up on the cross-bar of the bicycle, and Romi moved on again. He was quite used to carrying friends on the crossbar.

'Keep beating your milk-cans,' said Romi. 'Like that, the animals will know we are coming. My bell doesn't make enough noise. I'm going to get a horn for my cycle!'

'I never knew there were so many animals in the jungle,' said Teju. 'I saw a python in the middle of the road. It stretched right across!'

'What did you do?'

'Just kept running and jumped right over it!'

Teju continued to chatter but Romi's thoughts were on the

fire, which was much closer now. Flames shot up from the dry grass and ran up the trunks of trees and along the branches. Smoke billowed out above the forest.

Romi's eyes were smarting and his hair and eyebrows felt scorched. He was feeling tired but he couldn't stop now, he had to get beyond the range of the fire. Another ten or fifteen minutes of steady riding would get them to the small wooden bridge that spanned the little river separating the forest from the sugarcane fields.

Once across the river, they would be safe. The fire could not touch them on the other side because the forest ended at the river's edge. But could they get to the river in time?

4

Clang, clang, clang, went Teju's milk-cans. But the sound of the fire grew louder too.

A tall silk-cotton tree, its branches leaning across the road, had caught fire. They were almost beneath it when there was a crash and a burning branch fell to the ground a few yards in front of them.

The boys had to get off the bicycle and leave the road, forcing their way through a tangle of thorny bushes on the left, dragging and pushing at the bicycle and only returning to the road some distance ahead of the burning tree.

'We won't get out in time,' said Teju, back on the cross-bar but feeling disheartened.

'Yes, we will,' said Romi, pedalling with all his might. 'The fire hasn't crossed the road as yet.'

Even as he spoke, he saw a small flame leap up from the grass on the left. It wouldn't be long before more sparks and burning leaves were blown across the road to kindle the grass on the other side.

'Oh, look!' exclaimed Romi, bringing the bicycle to a sudden stop.

'What's wrong now?' asked Teju, rubbing his sore eyes. And then, through the smoke, he saw what was stopping them.

An elephant was standing in the middle of the road.

Teju slipped off the cross-bar, his cans rolling on the ground, bursting open and spilling their contents.

The elephant was about forty feet away. It moved about restlessly, its big ears flapping as it turned its head from side to side, wondering which way to go.

From far to the left, where the forest was still untouched, a herd of elephants moved towards the river. The leader of the herd raised his trunk and trumpeted a call. Hearing it, the elephant on the road raised its own trunk and trumpeted a reply. Then it shambled off into the forest, in the direction of the herd, leaving the way clear.

'Come, Teju, jump on!' urged Romi. 'We can't stay here much longer!'

5

Teju forgot about his milk-cans and pulled himself up on the cross-bar. Romi ran forward with the bicycle, to gain speed, and mounted swiftly. He kept as far as possible to the left of the road, trying to ignore the flames, the crackling, the smoke and the scorching heat.

It seemed that all the animals who could get away, had done so. The exodus across the road had stopped.

'We won't stop again,' said Romi, gritting his teeth. 'Not even for an elephant!'

'We're nearly there!' said Teju. He was perking up again.

A jackal, overcome by the heat and smoke, lay in the middle of the path, either dead or unconscious. Romi did not stop.

He swerved round the animal. Then he put all his strength into one final effort.

He covered the last hundred yards at top speed, and then they were out of the forest, free-wheeling down the sloping road to the river.

'Look!' shouted Teju. 'The bridge is on fire!'

Burning embers had floated down on to the small wooden bridge, and the dry, ancient timber had quickly caught fire. It was now burning fiercely.

Romi did not hesitate. He left the road, riding the bicycle over sand and pebbles. Then with a rush they went down the river-bank and into the water.

The next thing they knew, they were splashing around, trying to find each other in the darkness.

'Help!' cried Teju. 'I'm drowning!'

6

'Don't be silly,' said Romi. 'The water isn't deep—it's only up to the knees. Come here and grab hold of me.'

Teju splashed across and grabbed Romi by the belt.

'The water's so cold,' he said, his teeth chattering.

'Do you want to go back and warm yourself?' asked Romi. 'Some people are never satisfied. Come on, help me get the bicycle up. It's down here, just where we are standing.'

Together they managed to heave the bicycle out of the water and stand it upright.

'Now sit on it,' said Romi. 'I'll push you across.'

'We'll be swept away,' said Teju.

'No, we won't. There's not much water in the river at this time of the year. But the current is quite strong in the middle, so sit still. All right?'

'All right,' said Teju nervously.

Romi began guiding the bicycle across the river, one hand on the seat and one hand on the handlebar. The river was shallow and sluggish in midsummer; even so, it was quite swift in the middle. But having got safely out of the burning forest, Romi was in no mood to let a little river defeat him.

He kicked off his shoes, knowing they would be lost; and then gripping the smooth stones of the river-bed with his toes, he concentrated on keeping his balance and getting the bicycle and Teju through the middle of the stream. The water here came up to his waist, and the current would have been too strong for Teju. But when they reached the shallows, Teju got down and helped Romi push the bicycle.

They reached the opposite bank, and sank down on the grass.

'We can rest now,' said Romi. 'But not all night—I've got some medicine to give to my father.' He felt in his pockets and found that the tablets in their envelope, had turned into a soggy mess. 'Oh well, he had to take them with water anyway,' he said.

They watched the fire as it continued to spread through the forest. It had crossed the road down which they had come. The sky was a bright red, and the river reflected the colour of the sky.

Several elephants had found their way down to the river. They were cooling off by spraying water on each other with their trunks. Further downstream there were deer and other animals.

Romi and Teju looked at each other in the glow from the fire. They hadn't known each other very well before. But now they felt they had been friends for years.

'What are you thinking about?' asked Teju.

'I'm thinking,' said Romi, 'that even if the fire is out in a day or two, it will be a long time before the bridge is repaired. So it will be a nice long holiday from school!'

'But you can walk across the river,' said Teju. 'You just did it.'

'Impossible,' said Romi. 'It's much too swift.'

GUESTS WHO FLY IN
FROM THE FOREST

When mist fills the Himalayan valleys, and heavy monsoon rain sweeps across the hills, it is natural for wild creatures to seek shelter. Any shelter is welcome in a storm—and sometimes my cottage in the forest is the most convenient refuge.

There is no doubt that I make things easier for all concerned by leaving most of my windows open—I am one of those peculiar people who like to have plenty of fresh air indoors—and if a few birds, beasts and insects come in too, they're welcome, provided they don't make too much of a nuisance of themselves.

I must confess that I did lose patience with a bamboo beetle who blundered in the other night and fell into the water jug. I rescued him and pushed him out of the window. A few seconds later he came whirring in again, and with unerring accuracy landed with a plop in the same jug. I fished him out once more and offered him the freedom of the night. But attracted no doubt by the light and warmth of my small sitting-room, he came buzzing back, circling the room like a helicopter looking for a good place to land. Quickly I covered the water jug. He landed in a bowl of wild dahlias, and I allowed him to remain there, comfortably curled up in the hollow of a flower.

Sometimes, during the day, a bird visits me—a deep purple whistling-thrush, hopping about on long dainty legs, peering to right and left, too nervous to sing. She perches on the windowsill, looking out at the rain. She does not permit any familiarity. But if I sit quietly in my chair, she will sit quietly on her windowsill, glancing quickly at me now and then just to make sure that I'm keeping my distance. When the rain stops, she glides away, and it is only then, confident in her freedom, that she bursts into full-throated song, her broken but haunting melody echoing down the ravine.

A squirrel comes sometimes, when his home in the oak tree gets waterlogged. Apparently he is a bachelor; anyway, he lives alone. He knows me well, this squirrel, and is bold enough to climb on to the dining-table looking for tidbits which he always finds, because I leave them there deliberately. Had I met him when he was a youngster, he would have learned to eat from my hand; but I have only been here a few months. I like it this way. I am not looking for pets: these are simply guests.

Last week, as I was sitting down at my desk to write a long-deferred article, I was startled to see an emerald-green praying mantis sitting on my writing pad. He peered up at me with his protruberant glass bead eyes, and I stared down at him through my reading glasses. When I gave him a prod, he moved off in a leisurely way. Later I found him examining the binding of Whitman's *Leaves of Grass*; perhaps he had found a succulent bookworm. He disappeared for a couple of days, and then I found him on the dressing-table, preening himself before the mirror. Perhaps I am doing him an injustice in assuming that he was preening. Maybe he thought he'd met another mantis and was simply trying to make contact. Anyway, he seemed fascinated by his reflection.

Out in the garden, I spotted another mantis, perched on the jasmine bush. Its arms were raised like a boxer's. Perhaps they're a pair, I thought, and went indoors and fetched my mantis and placed him on the jasmine bush, opposite his fellow insect. He did not like what he saw—no comparison with his own image!—and made off in a huff.

My most interesting visitor comes at night, when the lights are still burning—a tiny bat who prefers to fly in at the door, should it be open, and will use the window only if there's no alternative. His object in entering the house is to snap up the moths that cluster around the lamps.

All the bats I've seen fly fairly high, keeping near the ceiling as far as possible, and only descending to ear level (my ear level) when they must; but this particular bat flies in low, like a dive bomber, and does acrobatics amongst the furniture, zooming in and out of chair legs and under tables. Once, while careening about the room in this fashion, he passed straight between my legs.

Has his radar gone wrong, I wondered, or is he just plain crazy?

I went to my shelves of *Natural History* and looked up Bats, but could find no explanation for this erratic behaviour. As a last resort, I turned to an ancient volume, Sterndale's *Indian Mammalia* (Calcutta, 1884), and in it, to my delight, I found what I was looking for:

> ...a bat found near Mussoorie by Captain Hutton, on the southern range of hills at 5,500 feet; head and body, 1.4 inch; skims close to the ground, instead of flying high as bats generally do, Habitat, Jharipani, N.W. Himalayas.

Apparently the bat was rare even in 1884.

Perhaps I've come across one of the few surviving members of the species: Jharipani is only two miles from where I live. And I feel rather offended that modern authorities should have ignored this tiny bat; possibly they feel that it is already extinct.

If so, I'm pleased to have rediscovered it. I am happy that it survives in my small corner of the woods, and I undertake to celebrate it in prose and verse.

THE SNAKE

When, after days of rain,
The sun appears,
The snake emerges,
Green-gold on the grass.
Kept in so long,
He basks for hours,
Soaks up the hot bright sun.
Knowing how shy he is of me,
I walk a gentle pace,
Letting him doze in peace.
But to the snake, earth-bound,
Each step must sound like thunder.
He glides away,
Goes underground.
I've known him for some years:
A harmless green grass-snake,
Who, when he sees me on the path,
Uncoils and disappears.

THE OWL

At night, when all is still,
The forest's sentinel
Glides silently across the hill
And perches in an old pine tree.
A friendly presence his!
No harm can come
From a night bird on the prowl.
His cry is mellow,
Much softer than a peacock's call.
Why then this fear of owls
Calling in the night?
If men must speak,
Then owls must hoot—
They have the right.
On me it casts no spell:
Rather, it seems to cry,
'The night is good—all's well, all's well.'

TO SEE A TIGER

M r Kishore drove me out to the forest rest house in his jeep, told me he'd be back in two days, and left me in the jungle. The caretaker of the rest house, a retired Indian Army corporal, made me a cup of tea.

'You have come to see the animals, sir?'

'Yes,' I said, looking around the clearing in front of the house, where a few domestic fowls scrabbled in the dust. 'Will I have to go far?'

'This is the best place, sir,' said the caretaker. 'See, the river is just below.'

A stream of clear mountain water ran through a shady glade of sal and sheesham trees about fifty yards from the house.

'The animals come at night,' said the caretaker. 'You can sit in the verandah with a cup of tea, and watch them. You must be very quiet, of course.'

'Will I see a tiger?' I asked. 'I've *come* to see a tiger.'

'Perhaps the tiger will come, sir,' said the caretaker with a tolerant smile. 'He will do his best, I am sure.'

He made me a simple lunch of rice and lentils, flavoured with a mango pickle. I spent the afternoon with a book taken from the rest house bookshelf. The small library hadn't been touched for over twenty years, and I had to make my choice from Marie Corelli, P.C. Wren, and early Wodehouse. I plumped for a Wodehouse—*Love Among the Chickens*. A peacock flaunted its tail feathers on the lawn, but I was not distracted. I had seen plenty of peacocks.

When it grew dark, I took up my position in the verandah, on an old cane chair. Bhag Singh, the caretaker, brought me dinner on a brass thali, with two different vegetables in separate katoris. The chapattis came in relays, brought hot from the kitchen by Bhag Singh's ten-year-old son. Then, sustained by more tea, sweet and milky, I began my vigil. It took an hour for Bhag Singh's family to settle down for the night in their outhouse. Their pi-dog stood outside, barking at me for half an hour, before he, too, fell asleep. The moon came up over the foothills, and the stream could be seen quite clearly.

And then a strange sound filled the night air. Not the roar of a tiger, nor the sawing of a leopard, but a rising crescendo of noise—wurk, wurk, wurk—issuing from the muddy banks near the stream. All the frogs in the jungle seemed to have gathered there that night. They must have been having a sort of Old Boys' Reunion, because everyone seemed to have something to say for himself. The speeches continued for about an hour. Then the meeting broke up, and silence returned to the forest.

A jackal slunk across the clearing. A puff of wind brushed through the trees. I was almost asleep when a cicada burst into violent music in a nearby tree. I started, and stared out at the silver, moon-green stream; but no animals came to drink that night. The next evening, Bhag Singh offered to sit up with me. He placed a charcoal burner on the verandah, and topped it with a large basin of tea.

'Whenever you feel sleepy, sir, I'll give you a glass of tea.'

Did we hear a panther—or was it someone sawing wood? The sounds are similar, in the distance. The frogs started up again. The Old Boys must have brought their wives along this time, because instead of speeches there was general conversation, exactly like the natter of a cocktail party.

By morning I had drunk over fifteen cups of tea. Out of respect for my grandfather, a pioneer tea planter in India, I did not complain. Bhag Singh made me an English breakfast—toast, fried eggs and more tea.

The third night passed in much the same way, except that Bhag Singh's son stayed up with us and drank his quota of tea.

In the morning, Mr Kishore came for me in his jeep.

'Did you see anything?'

'A jackal,' I said.

'Never mind, you'll have better luck next time. Of course, the jungles aren't what they used to be.'

I said goodbye to Bhag Singh, and got into the jeep.

We had gone barely a hundred yards along the forest road when Mr Kishore brought the jeep to a sudden, jolting halt.

Right in the middle of the road, about thirty yards in front of us, stood a magnificent full-grown tiger.

The tiger didn't roar. He didn't even snarl. But he gave us what appeared to be a quick, disdainful glance, and then walked majestically across the road and into the jungle.

'What luck!' exclaimed Mr Kishore. 'You can't complain now, can you? You've seen your tiger!'

'Yes,' I said. 'Three sleepless nights, and I've seen it in broad daylight!'

'Never mind,' said Mr Kishore. 'If you're tired, I know just the thing for you—a nice cup of tea.'

I think it was Malcolm Muggeridge who said that the only real Englishmen left in the world were to be found in India.